"My God, it's not you."

The man stared at her, his gaze measuring. "It's close...." Once again he studied the picture, then carefully searched her face. "Really close. But no cigar. What do you know about this woman? What did you call her...Terry? Where can I find her?"

Nina nearly let out a laugh, but it would have been half-hysterical, so she put her hand to her mouth and shook her head.

"I need to talk to her."

"You...can't," she said, wishing for something to rescue her from this nightmare.

"Why not?"

"She died last September."

His frown deepened. "Try again, lady."

Nina shook off the fear and found her temper. "I don't know who you are, but there is a guard right inside, and—"

"Don't call him. I just want some answers. I need to talk to her."

"No." Terry was dead.

And she needed to remain so.

Everything depended on her remaining so.

Jill Shalvis has been making up stories since she could hold a pencil. Now, thankfully, she gets to do it for a living, and doesn't plan to ever stop. Jill is a bestselling, award-winning author of over two dozen novels who has hit the Waldenbooks bestsellers lists, is a 2000 RITA® Award nominee and a two-time National Readers' Choice Award winner. Jill's first single title, *The Street Where She Lives,* appeared last October and she is hard at work on a new one.

TRUEBLOOD, TEXAS

JILL SHALVIS

Hero for Hire

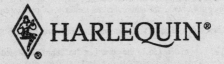

HARLEQUIN®

TORONTO • NEW YORK • LONDON
AMSTERDAM • PARIS • SYDNEY • HAMBURG
STOCKHOLM • ATHENS • TOKYO • MILAN • MADRID
PRAGUE • WARSAW • BUDAPEST • AUCKLAND

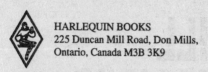

HARLEQUIN BOOKS
225 Duncan Mill Road, Don Mills,
Ontario, Canada M3B 3K9

ISBN 0-373-21743-9

HERO FOR HIRE

Copyright © 2001 by Harlequin Books S.A.

Jill Shalvis is acknowledged as the author of this work.

Visit us at www.eHarlequin.com

Printed in U.S.A.

Dear Reader,

I've written over two dozen novels, and this one,
Hero for Hire, was my favorite. Okay, so I say
that about every book I finish.

Nina Monteverde has a few secrets, one of which
is that she's never trusted a soul to see the real Nina.
Rick Singleton hates secrets. He's a dangerous, edgy,
brooding bounty hunter still paying for the one fatal
mistake that changed his life. When they are forced
by circumstances to work together, sparks fly.

So does a very unwelcome heat between them, a
heat that deepens quickly both in sultry Rio de Janeiro
and the untamed Amazon jungle, becoming the most
terrifying thing of all: love.

I love to hear from readers. You can write me
at P.O. Box 3945, Truckee, CA 96160-3945.
For a complete list of my books, please visit
www.eHarlequin.com or www.jillshalvis.com.

Thanks, and happy reading!

Jill Shalvis

PROLOGUE

FRUSTRATION BOILED UP *inside, crawling, screaming to be let out.*

What to do?

It should **be** *so simple. There were only three things* wor**th ha**ving *in life—wealth, power and physical beauty.*

Yet none had been obtained, which fried the blood. Others had gotten what they wanted. Others like Terry Monteverde.... Now there was a woman who'd had it all and hadn't even noticed. She'd lived her wild, wanton life without a single care.

Shameless.

She'd been punished for that, and that punishment had been quite satisfactory.

Only that satisfaction hadn't lasted long, not when the family reputation and success lived on through Terry's younger sister.

Nina Monteverde. Sweet and lovely. Beloved by all.

Just thinking about it had the bitterness and fury

burning inside all over again. The Monteverdes had everything, everything worth coveting.

Yet they were untouchable.

If only Terry was still alive to pay for her sins once again.

Since she wasn't, Nina would have to do.

CHAPTER ONE

MAN, THE HEAT was brutal. But then again, the weather in Rio de Janeiro was known for being brutal, even in the winter month of July.

Winter being relative of course, especially in the tropics.

Though the air came off the ocean and should have been cool, it wasn't; but after four years in Brazil, Rick Singleton considered himself a *Carioca*—a native—and hardly felt a thing.

In truth, he hardly felt anything anymore, and that was how he liked it. He'd definitely come to fit into the South American way of life, where everything was casual, come-what-may, and absolutely pleasure-based.

Not many would consider their job pleasure-based, but Rick did. As a bounty hunter, he lived for the thrill of the chase—not to mention the money he got paid for finding his man.

Or in this case, *woman*.

Reaching into his pocket, he pulled out the hazy

Polaroid of a couple taken two Carnivals back. The woman with her feathery mask had eyes only for the man holding her close. They looked excited, anticipatory, and given the man's hot gaze, they were headed for a night of passion.

Rick didn't know the woman's name. All he knew was that Mitch Barnes, the man in the picture, had hired him through Finders Keepers, a private investigation agency in Texas, to find her. They'd spent one night together, she and Mitch, and the man was desperate, evidenced both by the ridiculous amount of money he'd offered Rick, and the tone of his voice when he talked about his mystery woman.

He obviously cared a great deal about her.

Given the hordes of tourists that came to Brazil every year to partake in Carnival's decadent celebration, Rick doubted the woman even lived in Rio, but for the money he'd do his best to find her. He had no clues other than the elaborate necklace she wore.

Mitch, an injured and recovering FBI agent now living in San Antonio, hadn't known anything about the hand-wrought gold-and-emerald necklace, except that the woman looked gorgeous in it. Apparently their one night together had produced more than just a wild heat and passion. It had also produced a baby, a fact Mitch hadn't been aware of until he'd discovered the baby girl left on his neighbor's doorstep was his.

Now more than ever Mitch wanted to find the woman.

That was Rick's job. Not much to go on, but he'd worked on less. He hadn't screwed up a case since his ultimate failure four years prior.

Four years.

It was hard to believe it had been so long, and if there'd been any emotion left in him, any at all, he'd ache at the memory.

But his heart was as good as dead. Nothing got to him, not anymore.

He'd find the missing woman, no matter what he had to do, then get paid and move on. No sweat.

No looking back.

To that end, he stood in the middle of a particularly seedy *favela,* one of Rio's many shanty towns, where one fifth of the population crammed together, struggling daily just to scrape by. The run-down cities within a city sat precariously perched on the steep hillside on either side of Rio, seemingly poised to slide down the sharp cliffs. Contrary to Rio itself, which arguably had the most gorgeous vistas in all the world, there was little beauty to be found here.

Rick stared down would-be pickpockets and petty thieves, knowing the first law in a place like this was to see nothing and hear nothing.

And keep out of trouble.

If someone pulled a gun, or even a knife, he was on his own, as all government law and order stopped at the entrance to most favelas. Having been first a Navy SEAL and then a federal marshal in another life, Rick wasn't concerned. He could take care of himself.

"I'm looking for a woman," he said in Portuguese to his informant, Juan, a well-known fence and all-around low-life con artist who'd sooner sell his own mother than go to jail for his petty crimes.

"A woman?" Juan shoved his hands into his pockets and spoke in heavily accented English. "There's millions of people in Brazil, half of them women. Pick one."

"This one." Rick held out the picture Finders Keepers had sent him.

Juan stared at it. "Nice."

"Do you know her?"

"I didn't mean the woman." Juan let out a crusty laugh that told Rick he'd been smoking at least half his life. "The necklace. It's similar to *O Coração de Amante*."

"The what?"

Juan rolled his eyes. "The Lover's Heart," he said in English. "The original is in a museum somewhere, but clever remakes are popular with the *riqueza*. You know, the wealthy." He pulled the photo closer. "Either way, it's a very rare piece." He scratched his chin, eyes shining with speculation. "One could get rich off a piece like that, if it's real."

Given the woman's aristocratic beauty and dress, Rick doubted the necklace was anything but genuine. If he could trace it... "Where would I get another like it?"

"Ah, now you're talking."

"I mean legally."

"Oh." He sighed with disappointment. "Well, I'd bet my entire day's take—" He faltered at the steely, very hard cop look Rick shot him. "Er, I mean my week's *salary*, man. Salary. I'm not on the take—"

"The necklace, Juan."

"If it's the real deal, it came from the Monteverde's."

"Monteverde's?"

Face carefully blank, Juan held out his hand, palm up.

Rick swore, searched his pockets, then slapped some *reals* into Juan's outstretched palm.

Juan pocketed the money and held out his hand again. "Try American dollars. They go further."

"It had better be good," Rick warned, going back to his wallet.

"Always."

When Rick greased his palm with more bills, American this time, Juan gave him a grin that was missing more than one tooth. "Monteverde is the name of a famous Brazilian gem family. They have a huge business. An entire building in Ipanema, right on the beach. You might have seen it, it's the ritziest place out there. All That Glitters. They cater to people with too much money on their hands."

"Yeah." Rick rarely spent time in Rio's money belt. "Thanks. Stay clean, Juan."

"Sure," he vowed before slinking off.

Rick let him go, thinking with any luck he'd find the mystery woman by the end of the day and have a nice, fat wallet. Even better, he could be on another case by this time tomorrow. He straddled his motorcycle and drove down the steep, unpaved hills of no-man's-land, leaving the dark alleys of the *favela* behind. Within five minutes he drove into another world entirely, where throngs of people walked beautiful beaches half-nude, laughing, talking, running, playing without a care.

Surrounded by tall, majestic mountains, the ocean bay glittered a brilliant azure blue, its beaches made so scenic by palm trees and tropical flowers.

High above on the closest mountain peak towered a 130-foot statue of Christ, arms nearly as wide as he was tall, looking down on one and all, sinners and saints. The scene never failed to give Rick a cynical smile.

All That Glitters was indeed a huge business. It occupied one of the dozens of buildings crammed right on the beach, though it was bigger and better than most.

All eighteen floors of it.

While Rick debated the best plan of action, he parked and sat at an open *boteco*—Rio's answer to the American café—where he could watch the comings and goings, of which there were plenty.

The bottom floor of All That Glitters was an upscale jewelry retail store, where he assumed the Monteverde family sold what they had designed on the other seventeen floors. As he sat back to watch the goings-on through the store window, he caught sight of her.

The mystery woman.

In disbelief, he pulled out the worn photo. Same color chestnut hair, wild and full, though now the sides were slicked back with glittery combs. Same light-olive skin, smooth and flawless.

She turned then, and through the glass and the fifteen feet of hustling, bustling street that separated them, their gazes met.

And the oddest thing happened. She seemed to see him, really see him. *Him.* Something deep inside Rick jerked and came to attention at that.

It bothered him.

As a man for hire, one who'd effectively walked away from his own life, there was no one who knew or cared about him, and he liked it that way. People wanted him only for what he could do, and he liked that too, as frankly, there was little he *wouldn't* do. He'd purposely built a reputation as being the best bounty hunter in all of Brazil, and he never got personally involved with a case.

Not ever again.

No one touched his emotions, which he'd buried so far deep down he was certain they no longer existed.

No one.

But this woman... One look at her, just one meeting of the eyes, and he felt something inside him crack and soften.

It had to be the sun.

Or the crowd. There were millions of people in

Rio and he felt as if all of them were walking up and down this very street, showing off their youth, their bodies, their indifference.

Or maybe it was his busy schedule and lack of sleep. Since he took every case that came his way, no matter how difficult, and rarely hit dreamland easily, it was entirely possible.

Anything but a personal connection. Narrowing his gaze, he forced a cool, hard detachment, one he was terrifyingly good at, and got back to business.

Surveying her.

She was average weight and build, or so he assumed, since she'd hidden nearly every inch of her body behind a business suit that didn't fit into the Brazilian wear-as-little-as-possible way of life. She was still behind the counter, and with a visible shake, broke eye contact with him and turned to talk to another woman. With a shy smile and a light pat on the other woman's arm, his mystery woman disappeared into the back of the store.

She hadn't looked at him again.

Rick let out a long, slow breath, but before he could clear his head, a waitress came up to his table. She was dressed in a skimpy little skirt that sat low-slung on her hips and a bathing suit top designed to cover only her nipples—barely. Her crooked smile was both friendly and speculative. "Something to drink?" she asked in Portuguese, and when it took him a moment to pull his thoughts from across the street, she added in the bold way of Brazilian women, "Or...something else perhaps?"

Women had come on to him plenty of times, and plenty of times he'd appreciated it, but at the moment he was distracted. "Have you been in there?" he asked, gesturing across the street.

Laughing wryly, she shook her head. "Too pricey for the likes of me. But I've window-shopped plenty."

Window-shopped.

Yeah, that was it. He was going window shopping.

GRABBING HER PURSE, Nina Monteverde headed out. She was desperately in need of lunch, though it was already late afternoon. She'd skipped breakfast, and now that she thought about it, she'd skipped dinner the night before as well.

Her head throbbed with it.

Running All That Glitters was going to kill her. Second quarter paperwork was due, there were taxes to handle and several key employee contracts had come up for negotiation.

Terry could have handled all of it and more, with a bright smile.

At the thought of her beloved sister, Nina's throat tightened. The weight in her chest seemed to double. Triple.

But she kept walking, relieved to find a small table available at the café across the street. Grateful, she sat down and ordered. When her drink came, she sipped it, acknowledging the burning sensation behind her eyes as exhaustion, and promised herself that tonight she'd sleep.

No more nightmares.

Even if today was—*would* have been—Terry's birthday. Her sister should be home preparing her own celebration, just as she always had, and doing it in the outgoing, outrageous style in which she'd done everything.

Instead of being dead.

"Here, *cara*," the waitress said, setting a sandwich on the table. Then she plopped into the empty chair and grinned. "Break time for me, too. Whew, it's hot."

"It is only eighty degrees, Maria."

"Yes, but this is supposed to be winter. So—" she leaned close, studying Nina carefully "—you look…off today."

Yes, she was off. Hard to believe she could be

surrounded by people all day long and still feel…lonely. But Nina had been holding people at bay all her life, never really letting anyone in, and she'd gotten good at it.

Too good.

Maybe she regretted that now, that distance, but it was a hard habit to break.

"Nina?" Maria frowned in concern. "What's up?"

"It has been a long day, that is all." A long day fussing with the business end of things instead of designing, as her heart craved.

"You need to get laid," Maria decided.

Nina choked on her drink. She enjoyed Maria's company but she'd never gotten used to her friend's easy way of sharing absolutely everything. "I am fine."

"You're always fine." Sighing lustily, ignoring the tourists at the next table who were gesturing for her attention, Maria put her feet up and leaned back. "Don't you ever get tired of being so… fine?"

Actually, yes, Nina did get tired of it, of putting on the perfect, good-girl facade, not that she'd ever say so. After all, she'd been raised as the obedient, younger, seen-but-not-heard daughter. At twenty-six, that was a very difficult habit to break, even with the entire family business now firmly on her shoulders. "You have customers waiting."

"Oh, please. I'm not falling for that weak change of subject. Now talk. About *you*," she added pointedly. "And by the way, you know how I'm always bugging you to get a man?"

"They do not grow on trees. It is just not that easy for me."

"It should be. You're rich, you run a huge company, and you're beautiful. What wouldn't a man like?"

Exactly. It was all about money, prestige and looks, never about Nina as a person. She objected to that, and had learned to be alone instead.

She'd even learned to like it.

Mostly.

"Anyway, listen." Maria lowered her voice. "There's been a gorgeous guy here two days in a row, looking at you through the window of the shop."

"Be serious."

"I am." Maria dropped her feet and leaned in close. "I'll even point him out to you. He's a few tables over as we speak, watching you very carefully."

"Maria—"

"Shhh. He's tall, dark and dangerous. Got a

brooding edge to him, that one does. No, don't look! Not yet. *Meu Deus,* he's got a body, too, all muscle and hunger.''

Nina found herself reeled in. ''What does he look like?''

''He's wearing dark, unassuming clothes and looks like a man who knows what he wants and how to get it. Ah, and those eyes! Did I tell you about his eyes? They're spitfire green and full of heat. Now slowly crane your neck and look off to your right. See? Look at him look at you. *Magnifico!*'' Maria fanned herself wildly. ''Isn't he wicked?''

Wicked didn't begin to describe him. He was indeed all muscle and hunger and fire and heat, one-hundred percent of it directed right at Nina, who could suddenly scarcely breathe.

He was the man who'd held her gaze prisoner the day before when she'd innocently looked up and caught him watching her through the window. Her heart had thrown itself against her rib cage.

She hadn't liked it then. She didn't like it now either, though he had managed the one thing no one else had in days...he'd taken her mind off Terry.

''A man like that...'' Maria spoke in a hushed,

reverent whisper. "He knows how to satisfy a lover, no?"

Nina tried to tear her gaze away, tried to pull back, but there was something in his startling eyes that once again held her utterly captive. He didn't blink or look away, and she found she couldn't, either.

"*Americano?*" Maria wondered.

If he was indeed American, it was impossible to tell. Not all drop-dead gorgeous men were American. His sun-bleached brown hair and brilliant green eyes could have come from anywhere. His clothes were nondescript, yet emphasized his long, sculpted frame. His face, tanned and rugged and sporting at least a day's growth of beard, couldn't be pinpointed to any one nationality.

One thing was certain, she *had* definitely drawn his interest. Those searing eyes looked right at her. *Through* her. And though he certainly couldn't see inside—no one could—she felt as if he could read her thoughts.

They hadn't met, so he wasn't interested in her intellect, wit or personality. It couldn't be her exciting reputation either, since, unlike her sister, she didn't have one.

But men—specifically fortune hunters—didn't much care about Nina's looks or personality, and if this man was indeed a fortune hunter, he wouldn't be the first. She'd deal with him. She was in just the mood to do it. "I need to go."

"But your lunch."

"Bag it for me?"

"Nina—"

"Please?"

Maria tilted her head in the man's direction. "I think he wants to talk to you."

"I am not interested." To prove it, she wrenched her gaze from his, grabbed her purse and started across the street.

Not interested.

A lie, of course. She was interested, desperately so. Interested in learning what she'd missed in life by hiding away, by letting work take over, by letting family loyalty keep her silent.

The familiar spurt of bitterness went through her. After an overprotective childhood, not to mention growing up in the shadow of her sister's outrageous stunts, she'd purposely interacted with very few people, and certainly few strangers.

Much as she'd like to change things and start…well, living, she wasn't sure how to do that. And anyway, it didn't matter. Certainly the stranger, gorgeous as sin and likely double the trouble, had forgotten her already. She was positive of it.

So positive she didn't look back.

Though she wanted to.

THE REST OF the day flew by as she plowed through her business chores so she could get to her own private pride and joy—creating jewelry from her own designs.

It was her life, her heart, and once at her worktable, away from all the dreaded paperwork, she let her mind flow and empty, and she did what she did best—design original jewelry to go with the gems All That Glitters mined, purchased and traded all over the globe.

It was a quiet job, and one she did alone, which only perpetuated her reserved image. But she loved it more than anything, and wished she had more time for it these days.

Terry, I miss you, so much.

But what was done was done, and Nina had dealt with her grief. She'd dealt with the business. She'd truly moved on.

It just seemed her heart hadn't quite gotten the message yet. Determined to lighten her mood, if only for a little while, she adjusted her light and reached for her latest drawing, a bracelet of inlaid gold with emeralds. It would match the *Coração de Amante* she'd made for Terry several years ago. Already Nina knew she couldn't let this new piece go to sale. She'd dip into her own savings to buy it for herself.

She began by making a bezel, a gold sheet to hold the gems. For the next few hours she worked annealed gold around the stones, measuring, cutting and soldering with gold hard solder. By the time she stood up and stretched, it was long after dark, and the building was empty except for security.

She'd forgotten, if only for a while, her unbearable sadness.

Yes, tonight she'd sleep dream-free.

She was halfway across the back parking lot, heading toward her car, planning which book she'd take to bed with her to read until sleepiness overcame her, when she heard a footstep. A shadow fell over her.

Heart leaping, she whirled around.

And faced *him*. Her perfect stranger.

For one moment she had the ridiculous thought that he'd sought her out to ask her for a date.

How absurd. No one wanted her simply for herself. No one even *knew* the real her.

As she debated whether to stop or run, he pulled

a photo from his pocket and held it up. Comparing her to it, he glanced back and forth for a moment, then frowned before taking a step closer.

"Who are you?" he asked.

It should have been her question to him.

"*Como você se chama?* What's your name?" he tried in both Portuguese and English, still frowning.

If he'd been huge and menacing rather than lean and rangy as he was, he couldn't have been more intimidating. He stood over her, all lithe, tense muscle.

Maria was right, he was magnificent, one of the most magnificent men she'd ever seen, but that didn't make him any less dangerous.

Saying nothing, she backed up, wondering if she could make it to the building, where she could get help from the security guards within.

"Hey." He looked annoyed. "You speak Portuguese? English? What?"

"Both," she said, taking another step back.

"Don't run from me. I just want to talk to you." *Uh-huh. Right.*

Another step, though now she became uncertain about turning her back on him, because he looked athletic and fast as lightning, and she doubted her ability to outdistance him.

But if she screamed, would the security guards hear her from here?

"Stop," he demanded, yet he didn't reach for her, which she took as a good sign. "Just hold on a second, would ya?"

Nope. If he was going to rape, maim or murder her, he'd have to catch her first, and she didn't plan on being caught.

"I just want to know who you are," he said.

She hadn't lived in Rio all her life, but had been sent to private boarding schools in the United States, England and Switzerland. This man was indeed American, and southern American at that, given his slight drawl.

"Don't run." His voice was cool and quiet, but there was definite danger there. "And don't scream," he added. "I hate it when people scream. I just want to ask you some questions."

One more step, she thought, slowly lifting her foot, just…one…more.

"This picture." He thrust it beneath her nose. "What do you know about this picture?"

Foot in the air, poised for flight, Nina went utterly still. Her breath clogged in her throat. Her heart stopped.

It was her sister.

Meu Deus, he held a picture of Terry in the embrace of some man, and she looked so beautiful, so stunningly alive and happy, Nina's eyes filled. "Terry," she whispered.

The man stared at her. "My God, it's not you." His gaze was measuring. "It's close...." Once again he studied the picture, then carefully searched her face. "Really close." Before she could guess his intention, he reached up and unclipped her hair, tugging it free, ignoring her startled gasp. "But no cigar." His eyes, those all-seeing eyes, chilled. "What do you know about this woman? What did you call her...Terry? Where can I find her?"

Nina nearly let out a laugh, but it would have been half hysterical, so she put her hand to her mouth and shook her head.

"I need to talk to her."

For once, the streets were relatively free of the wandering tourists and loud boisterous locals. There was no one to rescue her from this bad dream. "You...cannot," she said.

"Why?"

"She died a year ago last September."

His frown deepened, his jaw tight as a drum. "Try again, lady."

Nina shook off the fear and found her temper. "I do not know who you are, but I want you to leave these premises immediately. There is a guard right inside, and—''

''Don't call him. I just want some answers. I need to talk to her.''

''No.'' Terry was dead.

And she needed to remain so.

Everything depended on her remaining so.

''How long since you've seen her?'' he pressed.

More than a year now. A lifetime. Nina closed her eyes and remembered the terror in her sister's face when she realized that she was being watched. Stalked. Then the police had come, arresting her for embezzlement and smuggling gems in cahoots with a known smuggling operation.

It had been a lie, a terrible, vicious lie. Terry had been set up and framed, but the evidence against her had been insurmountable. Planted, of course, though neither Terry nor Nina knew who would have done such a thing.

Nina still didn't know.

In light of that, while out on bail on charges that would put her in prison for life, Terry had vanished. Then she'd faked her own death, and Nina had grieved as if it had been the real thing, because she knew she'd never get to see Terry again.

''The waitress told me you were Senhorita Nina

Monteverde,'' the American said. ''If that's true, who's Terry?''

If this man was looking for her sister, something had gone terribly, terribly wrong, and Nina backed up another step.

''Maybe Terry is…your sister?''

Nina's eyes widened, she couldn't help it. He was good.

''Yeah,'' he said, nodding, still staring at her. ''Your sister. I need to talk to her, Nina.''

Another step.

Then another.

And yet another, all the while her brain frantically racing. *Terry, God, Terry please be all right.*

Then finally she had enough space between her and the American. ''Security!'' she shouted. ''Help! Security!''

Behind her the doors opened, and she whirled toward them, never so grateful for the wealth and status her family name afforded as two uniformed men rushed toward her. ''Escort this man off the premises!'' she cried, turning back to point out the American, as if he needed pointing out.

But the security men skidded to a halt, bafflement crossing their faces. Nina didn't understand, until she realized she pointed at nothing and no one.

Her stranger had vanished.

CHAPTER TWO

RICK WASN'T a patient man. One would think that worked against him in his line of work, but he'd found frustration and intimidation good motivators.

Only he'd blown it just now, letting Nina Monteverde stun him stupid with just one blink of those huge, wide, drown-in-me chocolate brown eyes.

What was that about?

He'd interviewed plenty of women in his day, and while it was true few could resist his own dubious charms, it had happened on occasion. But he'd still always gotten what he wanted.

Not tonight.

Tonight *he'd* been the one blindsided, and for his trouble all he'd gotten was a lie.

No way could the woman in the picture have been dead a year and a half. She'd given birth only seven months ago, then dumped the baby girl on what she thought was Mitch Barnes's doorstep.

Rick sat on his motorcycle contemplating his next move. He pulled out his cell phone, and without calculating the difference in the time zone, dialed Mitch's home.

"Barnes here."

"Does the name Monteverde mean anything to you?" Rick asked.

"No, why?"

"The woman in the picture, the one you're looking for, her name is Terry Monteverde."

"Terry." Mitch's voice, so professional and alert in his greeting, went rough with memories. "Terry Monteverde."

"Nina, her sister, claims she died last fall."

"That's a lie. I had a paternity test. Hope is mine. The only woman I was with at the right time was the woman in the picture."

"Yeah, Nina was lying. But I think she was protecting Terry, for whatever reason." Rick couldn't be sure why he thought so, he didn't know Nina Monteverde from Eve, but his instincts had never failed him. At least not in four years. "I'm going to follow her home and see what else I can get."

Across the miles and phone lines, Mitch swore softly. In the background, a baby was crying. "I know she's in some sort of trouble, I can feel it. It's the only reason she'd abandon her baby." He drew a deep breath. "She has to be found, she needs help."

"I'll find her." Rick could still see the parking lot of All That Glitters. Two armed guards escorted Nina to her car, where she looked around, craning her neck left and right.

Looking for him, Rick knew as she got in and started the car. "I'll get back to you," he said to Mitch, and clicked off, shoving the phone in his pocket. When she'd pulled away and could no longer hear him, he roared his bike to life.

Nina would lead him to Terry, he was certain of it, so certain he hurried to catch up, following Ms. Monteverde home.

Anything to keep his mind off the sound of Mitch's voice. That gruff, terrorized worry brought Rick far too close to the time when he could feel such things, too. To a time when he could still be disappointed by the people and circumstances in his life.

When he could still get hurt.

He'd done some hurting of his own, which would haunt him to his dying day.

He hadn't always been a bounty hunter. Once upon a time he'd grown up under the eye of his sweet, lovely mother, a woman who'd been deserted by his father while in labor with Rick. Poorer than dirt and alone in the world together, they'd done fine. Better than fine, actually. His mother had seen to it.

She'd gotten him through childhood before dying of breast cancer, but by then he had the basics down, her morals and love of life.

Everything was an adventure back then, wildly dangerous, and right up Rick's alley. He'd been untouchable in those days, and had thrived on it.

Until he'd met Mary Jo Anderson, the second sweet, lovely woman in his life, a witness he was charged to protect until she could testify in a murder case. With her help, they could bring down a very wanted man. If all went well, it was a case that would make everyone's career.

Rick was in his element. Until he looked into Mary Jo's wide, innocent eyes, that is.

Up to that point, he'd managed to go his entire life without sharing his heart. He'd shared his body plenty, but never anything else, so no one could have been more surprised when he fell for Mary Jo. It had softened him, and made him stupid. Careless.

But nothing could happen to her, not with Rick looking out for her, right? Oh yeah, he'd been a cocky son of a bitch.

And Mary Jo had been killed.

His fault. He hadn't been able to stop her murder, or protect her, though he'd sworn to both his country and Mary Jo to do exactly that.

Things had gone straight to hell in a handbasket after that. Destroyed, Rick had walked away from all he'd ever known, and spent months aimlessly wandering the globe, looking for trouble and often finding it. He'd finally ended up in Rio. Something about the sinful, wild, pagan city appealed to his troubled soul, and he'd been here ever since.

It had been four years, and thankfully he'd managed to bury those memories for good. Only in the occasional dream was he forced to relive them, and he'd awaken drenched in sweat and tears and remind himself that having no emotions and no heart was the only way to live.

It worked for him, allowed him to be the best bounty hunter there was, because without feelings, no one could touch him. He liked that.

Nina led him out of the ritzy business district and into the ritzy residential district, but as Rick stayed back far enough to remain anonymous, he realized something.

They weren't alone.

A low-profile sedan followed him following Nina, keeping well back, but definitely on their tail.

Normally, his adrenaline would have kicked in,

and so would the thrill of the chase and the highly anticipated victory.

His adrenaline did kick in, but oddly enough not the thrill. He didn't like the thought of someone else after Nina. It was the damn memories haunting him now, he knew. But he'd gone soft once, and as a result, had lost the dearest thing to him.

That could never happen again since he no longer had a heart, but as he drove through the starlit Rio night, Rick hit the gas pedal with an uneasy urgency.

THE FIRST THING Nina did inside her condo was lock and double lock her door. She had goose bumps up and down her limbs, and though she could have called any one of her father's men over to check on her, she felt silly.

The tough, brooding American was long gone, and she was safe.

As always, she raced to check her mail, hoping, praying… Flipping hurriedly through the bills and advertisements, she held her breath.

But no little letter from Baba, her old nanny, as arranged and promised through Terry. No news of her sister at all.

Nina sank to the couch, for once blind to the incredible view of the deep-blue bay spread out before her from floor-to-ceiling windows. She felt sick, and so tense she could have shattered.

Terry, whereever she was, had been sending twice monthly letters through Baba. Those letters said precious little, but they'd been all Nina had, and she'd treasured each one, hoarding it close to her heart for several hours before forcing herself to burn it.

She hadn't received one in over a month, and every day Nina grew more frantic.

Now there was an American asking around and he had a picture of Terry with a man she'd never seen.

It all combined to tell Nina the truth. Her sister was in trouble, even deeper trouble than being framed for embezzlement and smuggling gems.

Grabbing the phone, praying Rio's notoriously bad phone service was in order, Nina dialed Baba. She woke the poor woman up, and quickly asked the same question she'd been asking her almost nightly now for weeks.

"Any word?"

"Nada, minha amada."

Nothing, my sweetheart.

Baba didn't say more, but she didn't have to—it was all there in her voice, the fear, the worry. Nina hung up and tried to calm herself, but the feeling of dread continued to intensify. Something had happened, something had gone wrong.

What was she going to do?

The American kept popping into her head. How had he gotten that picture? And what did he want with Terry?

Would he just go away?

She wanted to think so, but despite appearances, she wasn't that naive. The man had been too focused, too intense for him to simply vanish without getting what he wanted.

And too extraordinary.

That she'd even noticed during those few moments of terror really disturbed her, but there was no denying there'd been something in his gaze, something deep and nearly hidden that had startled her.

Pain.

The realization rocked her, then made her laugh. The man had terrified her. Yet she'd bothered to notice his hidden pain.

She needed help, serious help.

A sound from the kitchen distracted her, and she went still for one second, before grabbing a fire poker from the fireplace she never used.

The only sound now was her own ragged

breathing as she tiptoed to the double swinging doors and peeked in.

Nothing.

She'd spooked herself, and just as she let the air out of her lungs, the phone rang, causing her to nearly leap out of her skin. With a hand to her chest, she shook her head at herself and picked up the receiver.

"Nina, the financials are due in the morning."

The gruff, no-nonsense, no greeting was typical of John Henry. He was second in command of All That Glitters, next to her.

It hadn't always been that way. Once upon a time, before she and Terry had been old enough to take the reins, John Henry had run the place for their invalid father.

And when their father had deemed the surprisingly business-savvy Terry old enough to take over, he'd removed the job from John Henry without qualm, leaving the fiercely ambitious man reporting to a woman he not so secretly felt was beneath him.

He'd never forgiven any of them for that, and Nina, the only one left to deal with him on a daily basis, got to face the brunt of his attitude. "The financials are complete," she said, ignoring his silent surprise that she'd done her job. She *always* did her job, sometimes at the expense of her own happiness, but that he expected her to fail, even wanted her to, hurt. "But thank you for your offer of help."

He ignored the dry quip. "Everything is good?"

The tall, stern, perpetually frowning man wasn't asking about her health or her life, she'd learned the hard way. On her first day, John Henry had asked her the same question, and at the thought that she was only there because Terry was dead and buried, she'd burst into tears.

John Henry had simply walked out of her office without a word, coming back when she'd composed herself.

"Everything is perfectly in balance," she said now.

"Did you include the paperwork your father had worked on during his last visit to Arraial do Cabo?" he asked.

"Yes, I—" Oh, no. The Monteverde vacation estate! Good Lord, how could she have so completely forgotten?

Nina had long ago gone through her sister's condo, burning everything and anything that could have been used against Terry. Correspondence, notes, journals, everything.

Illegal, yes, but Nina hadn't cared. Her sister

was innocent, framed for whatever reason, and the authorities had gone along with it, so all rules had been off as far as Nina was concerned. She'd have done far worse to protect her sister.

People thought of Nina as the good girl. *Ha!* If they only knew the fire she had burning deep within her, the fierce love and sense of loyalty she felt toward her family.

But she'd forgotten the vacation home she hadn't been to since Terry's "death." Who knew what her sister had out there that could be used to track her down.

"Nina?"

"Yes, John Henry," she said carefully. "I am here. And you are quite right, I had forgotten about the paperwork at the vacation estate."

His silence said volumes about what he thought of her first and only "mistake."

"In fact," she said trying to contain her sudden attack of nerves, "I need to drive up to Arrairal do Cabo myself. I will leave now and be back at the office by tomorrow afternoon the latest."

"If you insist."

He could have offered any one of a dozen minions to make the three-hour drive and handle the chore for her, but he didn't, and for once Nina was grateful John Henry was selfish and bitter and resentful.

She needed to go, and she needed to go alone.

NINA MADE THE TRIP into the mountains with nothing but her own nerves for company.

It was horrifying how the mind could play tricks. She imagined she was being followed. Imagined being kidnapped and tortured.

Imagined her sister dead for real.

But common sense came over her. First of all, no one knew where she was going besides John Henry, and while he was a cranky pain in her behind, he wouldn't do anything to hurt his precious job.

As for being followed, the road was so well traveled by both locals and tourists, even this late at night, that it would be nearly impossible for anyone to follow her, especially a gorgeous, brooding American not familiar with the winding highway.

Besides, she simply wasn't that important. Not to anyone, not anymore. Her father was housebound and cared for by his adoring servants. She visited him every other week, and while he appreciated her running All That Glitters, he didn't seem to need anything more from her.

Ah, that was it.

Self-pity.

She was feeling that strange, inexplicable lone-liness again, the sense that there was no one she could trust with the real Nina Monteverde.

With a skill that came from long years of practice, she pushed the feelings away. But when she pulled up to the family estate, the beautiful Spanish-style ranch that sprawled thirty acres over the mountainside, memories washed over her.

Here was where they'd spent many summers, she and her sister, watched over by servants and Baba. It hadn't been a hardship, because for the most part they'd been left alone to do as they pleased.

For Terry it had been sunbathing and boy gazing.

For Nina, it had been reading and *secret* boy gazing. She'd never had the nerve and splashiness of her sister, and now, given the life Terry had been forced to lead for the past year and a half, Nina should be content.

But the truth was, she'd always admired Terry for knowing what she wanted, for going after it with such complete abandon. To know Terry was to look at her. She'd worn her life and emotions on her sleeve for all to see.

No one could look at Nina and know her life's

ambitions, and certainly not her emotions. She'd been hiding them so long she wasn't even certain herself anymore who she really was.

Going inside, she carefully locked up behind her. Then, because it was so late and she felt more exhausted than she could ever remember feeling, she made her way directly to her bedroom.

She'd search the place first thing in the morning.

Yawning, she undressed. With one look out into the incredible night sky awash with millions of stars, their reflection dancing over the wild, dark mountains, her head hit the pillow and she was out.

SHE DREAMED BADLY, and as she tossed and turned, she attributed it to the fact she hadn't yet done what she'd come for.

God only knew what clues Terry had left in her hurry to escape Brazil, and now that someone was looking for her, Nina felt that urgency as her own.

But she finally fell into a deep sleep, this time dreaming of fire-green, searing eyes and the intense expression of the American's arresting face as he leaned toward her, over her, closer and closer with that long, beautifully formed body of his, until her breath backed up in her lungs.

Was he going to kiss her?

Was that why her body tingled in vibrant awareness, her pulse dancing and leaping as she arched closer?

His hands reached out, and she imagined them caressing her every inch, giving her pleasure such as she'd never known.

But instead they circled her neck and started to squeeze.

That's when she remembered, even deeply asleep, that the lean, edgy man wasn't just beautiful.

He was dangerous.

She needed to remember that, and promised herself she would as she shifted into a more normal sleep. She dreamed of Terry, of their happy, carefree childhood as a watchful part of her chased away the disturbing dreams.

And awakened with a silent scream when a hand covered her mouth.

"Where is she?"

Nina could see nothing, which added to her terror. Kicking out into the dark room, she found herself pinned to the mattress, a hard, powerful body stretched out over hers, her arms immobile above her head.

"Come on, Nina." He said the name slowly, purposely, in his very American way, and she knew instantly who held her so intimately. "Tell me."

Fear clouded her brain for a moment, before her rare temper took over and she remembered to use her knee forcefully.

A satisfying grunt sounded in her ear, but he recovered quickly, simply using his superior strength and weight to hold her still. "Hey! Careful!"

That he sounded more incredulous than angry didn't stop her from struggling, and though he was on to her now, she still gave him a good fight.

"Don't, damn it," he grated in her ear, doing his best to both hold her and fight her off, but her fear and temper had dulled her mind, and she fought him mindlessly, getting in one more carefully aimed knee before he pressed her hard into the mattress.

Lifting his head, chest heaving from the exertion, he spoke an inch from her mouth. "Lord, you're a squirmy little thing."

His skin was warm, his body hard with muscle. His weight wasn't uncomfortable, which disturbed her.

So did the way her body seemed to welcome his thigh thrust high between hers, forcing her legs open. Despite the confusing, mixed signals her brain sent, she continued to struggle. "Get off me!"

"Soon as you promise not to scratch my eyes out. Or other, more critical parts."

"I promise." She'd promise him the moon if he'd get off her.

He slanted her a doubtful gaze, then sighed the sigh of a martyr, as though *he* was the one being inconvenienced. "Look, your virtue is safe with me, all right? You're not even my type, so just relax and answer my questions."

Not only had he invaded her home and scared her half to death, but she was quite certain she'd just been insulted. *"Get off me!"*

"First tell me why you have two goons following you. Oh, and the question of the day, of course. *Where is your sister?"*

CHAPTER THREE

"THERE IS NO ONE following me but you!" Nina cried.

"Not anymore," Rick agreed. "Because once they saw you pull in here, they took off."

She stopped struggling for a second. "You... must be mistaken."

"And your sister?"

"I told you, she is dead."

Rick stared down into Nina's face, seeing the fear and fury, highlighted by the faint moonlight coming in the window.

Her fear bothered him. He knew he should reassure her he didn't rape and pillage for a living, but all he could think was...did she not realize he could see right through her? Everything about her, the wide eyes, the uneven breathing, the not quite direct eye contact—everything told him she was lying through her teeth.

He'd seen and done it all, and as a result knew most people were capable of deception. Maybe he'd turned cynical, yes, but he had good reason to be exactly who and what he was, down to his very toes.

All he knew was that this woman, sweet and lovely as she may be, had lied, because a woman who'd died a year and a half ago couldn't have given birth a couple of months later.

"Try again," he said, wanting this over with. Her lie wasn't the only thing getting to him. Every time he'd seen her in the two days he'd been staking out All That Glitters, she'd been fully dressed in colorful but modest business attire. Even her hair had been restrained.

But now…my God. Now she was the antithesis of that cool, elegant woman. Her chestnut hair sprawled across the pillow in silken waves, and also across his arm, which still held her hands over her head. It was long and thick and scented with some shampoo that made him want to lean in close and sniff some more.

And her body… Well, she most definitely had one. She wore a thin cotton T-shirt. No bra. And since she was pressed to him like shrink-wrap, he could feel her warm, full breasts, her nipples drilling holes into his chest. One arm of the shirt had slid off her shoulder in their tussle, revealing a smooth, tanned shoulder that he had the most ridiculous urge to bend down and bite.

And that was before he realized he lay between her spread thighs, having put himself in that erotic position during their struggle. Even worse, the hem of her T-shirt had tangled around her waist, revealing a pair of plain white cotton panties that suddenly seemed sexier than the most revealing lingerie.

She was amazing.

And her eyes spit bullets. He understood then that the restrained, almost prim woman he'd seen at work was a cover-up. A sham. There was nothing restrained or prim about her.

At the thought, his body reacted, and shoved up against the V of her opened legs as he was, he knew she could feel him. He forced himself to look into her face and found her staring up at him with a mixture of expressions all her own.

Horror.

And reluctant, befuddled arousal.

That made two of them, he thought grimly, pulling back enough that she could close her legs together, which she did so quickly that she slid against the front of his jeans, causing more torture.

At the helpless groan ripped from him, she closed her eyes.

He cleared his husky throat. "About your sister."

As she had before, she drove her knee up, and since he'd started to relax his hold, her aim was far more accurate this time, hitting him high on the inside of his left thigh. High enough to send stars dancing across his vision. The breath whooshed out of him and he swore the air blue.

Cringing back as far as she could go, Nina closed her eyes tighter.

And damn it, that little protective gesture made him feel like a jerk. "I told you I'm not going to hurt you. I just want the truth."

It should bother him, he supposed, that he was holding back plenty of truths himself. One, he feared Terry was in deep danger. Two, Mitch clearly imagined himself in love with her. And three, she'd left a baby on a doorstep in Texas.

But Nina probably knew all of that. And yet if that was true, why hadn't Terry left her baby with Nina?

There had to be a damn good reason for that, and until he knew it, baby Hope remained a secret.

"I do not have the truth you seek," Nina said in her formal but flawless English. "I have nothing for you."

He was used to that—there weren't many who

had much for Rick. But he no longer cared. "I'm not going anywhere." Deliberately, he lay more fully over her. "We can hang out all night, for all I care."

"My sister is dead," she whispered, her voice suddenly thick, which would have made him feel like an even bigger jerk if he hadn't known that to be a lie.

Terry wasn't dead. She'd just somehow managed to convince everyone else that it was true.

Question was, did Nina know that truth?

Right this very moment Mitch was probably holding the baby he and Terry had made together. Mitch believed Terry needed their help.

Rick didn't yet know what he believed, but he would learn the truth.

"Terry isn't dead," he said slowly. "I know it and you know it. So stop repeating yourself and tell me something that I can use."

"Why should I tell you anything?" She lifted her chin defiantly, though she still trembled beneath him. "I do not know who you are or what you want."

He had no idea if it was her forced bravado or the way she spoke English without using contractions, but he softened toward her, just a little. "Okay, I'll play. My name is Rick Singleton. I'm a bounty hunter. There. Now you know who I am and what I want."

"A bounty hunter." Her lips formed a perfect little O of distress. "You have been hired by the police to bring her back! But she is—"

"Dead. Yes, so you've said." He stared down at her, wondering why the police would be looking for Terry. He was definitely missing most of this puzzle. "Maybe *no one* is fooled, Nina. What do the police want her back for?"

"To go to jail, of course, on that phony embezzlement charge. But she was set up, framed!"

"So you helped her escape."

She closed her mouth.

"Maybe even helped her fake her death?"

"That would be against the law."

Ah, things were starting to click into place. Terry had gotten herself in trouble with the Brazilian law.

And had she indeed been framed, as her sister clearly believed, or had the wild older sister bitten off more than she could chew?

He'd have to check that out.

In the meantime, there was really no harm in letting Nina in on a few details, especially if it would ease her mind and loosen her tongue a little. "I'm not with the police. I was hired by Finders

Keepers, a private investigation service, to find your sister.'' He wouldn't say more now, not until he figured out what the hell was going on.

It seemed unlikely that this wide and wild-eyed innocent beauty could be tangled up in anything that would hurt Terry Monteverde, but Rick knew better than to blindly believe in anyone.

Proving that, Nina took advantage of his lax hold on her and rolled free of not only him, but the bed. When she tumbled to the floor, he dived after her, but she evaded him with a surprising agility and came to stand on the far side of the room, chest heaving, hair in her face.

They faced off like that for one split second, before she whirled and vanished out the door and down the hallway.

Damn it. With a sigh at her ignorance in thinking she could outrun him, he went after her, slamming his shin against a chest in her bedroom, then walking straight into the door, which she'd cleverly shut behind her.

Swearing, hopping on one foot, he started down the hallway after her, stopping only to pull a flashlight out of his pocket in order to avoid more injuries.

He had no idea how a little slip of a woman had gotten the best of him, but she definitely had, and it annoyed him. He'd gone easy on her—it had been those dark, mesmerizing eyes—but it wouldn't happen again.

Her white T-shirt glimmered up ahead and he went after that. The hallway opened up into a huge, open living room. One entire wall was glass, overlooking the mountain vista. Light from the moon and stars filtered in, aiding him in the chase.

Nina's shirt whipped up about her thighs, her bare feet flashing as they pumped, but he let her stay just ahead, hoping she'd exhaust herself. He couldn't see tumbling her down to the hardwood floor, and since there was no way she was getting away from him again, he began to enjoy both the chase and the view she unwittingly gave him.

Oh, yeah, he was definitely going to be a fan of plain white underwear in the future.

Then she vanished behind a door.

He burst through it and found himself blinking in the bright glare of the kitchen, staring down a wild-looking Nina wielding...a can of juice?

"Stay back!" she commanded.

He couldn't help it, he laughed. "Yeah, that'll protect you."

She looked so fierce holding her can. That T-shirt she wore was plain, white and stark. With her free hand she tugged on the hem, modestly pulling it tight across her chest in order to cover herself to midthigh.

He wondered what she'd say if he told her she'd made the shirt nice and sheer.

Oh, and that she was cold.

Somehow that damn shirt was the sexiest thing he'd seen, and yet innocence shimmered off her in waves.

He wanted to believe it was an act. After all, at work she'd been all suited up and reserved. But here, in bed and right now, she was rumpled and warm and absolutely, heart-joltingly beautiful.

"Why on earth," he said, talking before thinking, a dangerous condition at the best of times, "do you go to all the trouble it must take to hide yourself in those uptight clothes during the day?"

It obviously wasn't what she expected him to say. She went still as a rabbit for one heartbeat, before dropping the can and whirling toward the back door.

NINA DIDN'T get it opened; she didn't have a chance before he was there, his chest to her back, his arms reaching past hers to hold the door firmly closed.

"I'm guessing you don't want to talk about your dressing habits," he said in her ear.

Sagging, she put her forehead against the wood, but all that did was sandwich her between the hard door and the even harder body of her pursuer.

"How about we talk about your sister, then?" he asked calmly.

Enraged, terrified, she fought.

He let her. She knew he thought it funny, both her pathetic struggles and the can of juice she'd nearly lobbed at his head, and she couldn't stop picturing his wide, mocking grin.

All her life she'd been humored, and she resented it with every bit of her being. As a result, she continued to fight him like a wild cat.

He had no trouble keeping her pinned. When she tried to kick back, he simply pressed in closer, so close she could feel the power in his thighs, his belly, his chest. When she reached back instead, attempting to push him away, he ran his hands down her arms, manacling her wrists, holding them on either side of her head.

It infuriated her, both his superior strength and the way he used it against her. Refusing to give up, she kept fighting until finally she didn't have a breath left in her body.

"Ready to talk?"

"Let go, you are hurting me."

"If I let go, you'll hurt *me*."

As if she could! Making her feel even more insignificant, he didn't loosen his hold, but somehow gentled it so that his hands no longer hurt her, and her body, quivering with indignation and exhaustion, was supported by his.

She felt weak and vulnerable, and she resented that more than anything. "I hate you."

"Nothing personal, *senhorita*, but I'm not real fond of you myself."

"Then go away!"

"I can't. I've been hired to find your sister."

"You have already said. And as I have already said, she is dead. Are you short on memory?"

He let out one bark of laughter. "You're not much in a position to annoy me, Nina."

But she thought maybe she was. If he'd been planning to hurt her, he'd have done so by now. She was banking on it. All she had to do was wait until he lowered his guard and she'd... She'd figure that out when the time came.

Hopefully.

In the meantime she tried to block out the feeling of his entire body against hers like a layer of paint. It should have disgusted her, should have continued to stoke her temper, but something odd was happening, as it had in her bedroom. She felt warm, from the inside out, sort of itchy and tingly, and she didn't like it.

"Are you going to run again?" he asked.

"No."

"Are you just saying that so I'll back off?"

"Yes."

He let out another short laugh. "Okay, one point for honesty. But I'm tired, Nina. So don't push your luck." Slowly, he pulled back, but only a few inches. Just enough that she could whirl around and face him.

And realize he was still way too close, because all she could think of was…him.

"Back to Terry," he said, abruptly distracting her from the fact she knew that every inch of him was warm, hard and smelled like… Well, she hadn't had many opportunities to be plastered against a man like this, but she imagined his scent was pure male. In any case, it was startlingly, annoyingly good.

"Is she hiding at another Monteverde estate?"

She looked up into his moss-green eyes. "Someone must be paying you a lot of money." This was spoken bitterly, but she couldn't help it. "I assume you want the money or gems Terry has been accused of embezzling, but as she never stole a thing in her life, I hope you rot in hell trying to find it."

He didn't so much as blink. "How about we start with the fact that I know she's not dead. The two of you faked her death, right? So all you have to do is tell me where I can find her."

Now it was her turn to laugh, but unfortunately, it sounded more like a choked-off cry of dismay.

He frowned, eyes narrowed. "I want an answer."

"I do not have one for you."

His gaze ran down her face, over her body, and then slowly, slowly back up, making her vibrantly aware of how little she wore.

Crossing her arms, she retreated a step and came up against the door. "I mean it. You might as well go away. I cannot help you."

"*Won't,* you mean." He shrugged. "Never mind. I'll help myself." He started rifling through the kitchen. First the silverware drawer, the utensil drawer, and then he came to the universal place in most kitchens...the "junk" drawer.

"Hey," she protested as he searched through the various things in it. "Stop that."

Ignoring her, he picked up a pad of paper and started reading the scratched notes.

Nina had no idea what was on that pad, but as she hadn't yet gone through the house to destroy any possible clues to Terry's whereabouts, she couldn't let him continue. "Put that down!"

Without a word, he tossed the pad aside and headed toward the living room. Grabbing her can of juice back off the counter, she went after him, scooping up a throw blanket that had been tossed over one sofa. She wrapped it around her waist, wishing for the dubious protection of her clothes, but she didn't want to leave him alone in this room for even a moment. She came up behind him and lifted her can of juice.

He caught sight of her and let out an obnoxious grin. "You're tenacious for a sweet little thing, I'll give you that. Now put that down before you hurt yourself."

"I am going to hurt *you.*"

"No, you're not." Incredibly, he turned his back on her. "Did you know you don't use contractions? Is English your second or third language?"

She nearly screamed in frustration. She knew four languages fluently, as if he really cared! Coming up behind him, she once again hoisted the can over his head but hesitated. Never in her life had she physically hurt someone. She hadn't imagined it would be so difficult. But just as she promised herself she could do it, he stepped forward, out of range, searching the bookcase.

Nina threw a glance at the phone on the end table. She could call the police. *They'd* hurt him. Lifting the receiver, she watched Rick crane his neck and meet her gaze, and she smiled in triumph, until she realized…there was no dial tone.

Slamming down the phone, she faced his knowing grin. "I have a cell phone." She didn't say she'd left it in the car.

"Uh-huh." He went back to searching.

What if he found something?

What if it led him to Terry?

Her own fault. She should have already made a search and disposed of anything suspicious.

Ignoring her and her angst, Rick was blithely going through everything he came to—pictures, books, drawers, albums. Nina was such a small threat, he never even looked at her.

But she'd had it.

First her sister's birthday, which had gone unnoticed by all except her. She realized her father was an invalid now, but the truth was, unless it was his own birthday, he rarely bothered to remember such things.

But *she'd* remembered, and she ached. Her memories of Terry and all their celebrations over the years had brought back her grief fresh as the day Terry had vanished.

Now this man. Invading her home, her space, her privacy.

"I am going to my car to get my cell phone," she announced, and stormed past him.

"Yeah, do that. And while you're at it, why don't you tell them you're an accomplice to a woman who faked her death to get out of the charges against her, okay?" His eyes glittered with mockery, stopping her cold.

She couldn't go to jail; she had to be here to help Terry if she needed it.

"Well?"

Feeling trapped, she glared at him, but didn't go to her car.

Rick merely saluted her decision and went back to methodically searching her house, while she could only watch.

And pray he didn't find anything.

CHAPTER FOUR

THE RAGE was like a drug. It empowered. So did learning Nina Monteverde had fled town for her family's vacation estate.

Strange, that. Nina never fled anything. She was cool, calm and utterly professional at all times.

So what had happened?

The need to know burned.

This should have been the most satisfying time ever. Hadn't Terry been brought down, and brought down hard? Wasn't she dead and buried?

Yes!

So what was going on?

Something big. It could be felt to the bone.

"THERE IS NOTHING worth looking for in there," Nina said.

Rick looked up from the chest in the living room to where Nina stood over him, hovering. "Oh, and I believe you." He opened it, rummaging through a pile of sandals, tennis shoes, boots, all the while ignoring how the nervous Nina shifted back and forth, working her hands together.

What was she afraid he'd find?

Whatever it was, he *was* going to find it.

"Really, I have no idea why you would want to look through a bunch of dirty, old, stinky shoes. But if you must..." She shrugged as if it were of no concern to her, which was, of course, yet another big fat lie.

"Oh, I must." Beneath the shoes he found a stack of books. Yearbooks, to be exact, of boarding schools from all corners of the world, and one, looking somewhat out of place, from Northwestern University. "Switzerland, London, New York, Houston..." He looked up at her. "My, my, the Monteverde sisters were busy, weren't you?"

"We are well traveled, yes." Her nose was so high in the air now she was going to get a nosebleed.

He flipped through the one from Texas, watching Nina out of the corner of his eye. "Yours?"

She lifted a shoulder noncommittally.

She was a cool one, he'd give her that, but she had a way of giving away her every thought. When she bit her lip, he slowed down, taking a second glance at a bunch of pictures in the book. "Well, look at that,'' he said, staring at the page, wondering what the hell he was seeing at.

She was biting her lower lip so hard now it was colorless, so he took another good hard look.

And hit the jackpot. ''Is this you or Terry?'' he asked, pointing to a picture of two girls standing on a tennis court in whites, their arms around each other, their grins wide and cocky. One was a tall, leggy auburn beauty, the other... ''Terry,'' he guessed before Nina could answer. ''She's the one on the left. Her hair is slightly lighter than yours, and she wears far more makeup than I've ever seen you wear.''

''You have seen me only twice,'' she pointed out frostily.

He stared at the other girl, the one with auburn hair twisted into corkscrew curls and smiling hazel eyes. ''Who's this?''

''Her best friend.''

He flipped another couple of pages and came to one titled Most Likelys. The friend was there as Most Likely to Sail Around the World Under Her Own Power. ''An accomplished sailor, huh?''

He wasn't surprised at the lack of response.

Terry's picture showed her wearing a sexy, come-hither smile, a wild red outfit and more blatantly outrageous makeup. He wondered how he'd ever thought the two sisters looked alike. "Here's Terry again. Listed as Most Likely To Party Hardy."

Nina reached past him, shut the book and grabbed it out of his hands. Pressing it to her chest, she stood there with her eyes closed. When she opened them, they were blazing with…ah, hell.

Pain.

Even as he thought it, a tear formed on her long, dark lashes.

Rick had plenty of experience with women, but most of it related to a horizontal position. Even his life with Mary Jo had been far too hot too fast, and then before he could even blink, she'd been dead.

And so had his heart.

If he tried really hard he could remember his mother crying occasionally, but that had always been a private thing, where she'd lock herself in the bathroom, have a good pity party, and then come out with a smile.

As a result, tears mystified him.

Terrified him. "Don't even think about crying."

She sniffed.

"Stop that."

"I miss her," she whispered, then turned away.

"I'm sorry," he heard himself say, more surprised to realize he meant it.

For one brief second in time, she hesitated. Then she straightened her shoulders, adjusted the blanket around her hips, and kept moving.

So did he. The living room had been thoroughly searched, and while the yearbook had been an interesting diversion, he needed to move on.

He needed something that would lead him to Terry Monteverde. So he followed Nina, startled when she abruptly opened a door and stepped aside, standing there with her eyes still shining suspiciously, the yearbook clasped tightly to her chest.

"What is it?" he asked.

"The bedroom Terry used. If you're going to search, you can start here."

"All right." He waited warily, wondering at this sudden show of hospitality.

"I am going back to bed."

He'd turned away, stepping into the rather spartan bedroom, when instinct made him look back.

Little Miss Helpful Nina Monteverde was not going back to her bedroom, she was entering yet another door off the hallway and shutting it behind her.

Damn it!

When he hauled it open a second later, she whipped around, eyes huge. "You scared me."

"I should." He stalked toward her, toward the

chest at the foot of the bed that she'd been just about to open. "What's in there?"

Instead of backing away, as he imagined she would, she drew the blanket around her like a queen gathering her robe, and lifted her chin. "Nothing."

"If it's nothing, why are you so desperate for me to leave?"

The pulse at the base of her neck drummed wildly.

"I thought you were going to bed," he said.

"I was."

"This isn't the bedroom I found you in, Nina."

"I...like to trade off."

"Uh-huh." The walls were bright yellow, the bed coverings leopard print. Unlike Nina's conservative, nearly all white bedroom, which had held only a bed, a dresser and a wicker chair, this bedroom had a huge vanity table, every inch covered with bottles and stoppers and makeup galore.

"It is true. Look." Nina plopped on the bed, and when the blanket around her hips gave away, exposing her thighs, she scrambled to cover herself.

A damn shame, he thought. It should be illegal to hide a set of legs like that, all toned and tanned—

"I am going to sleep right here." She stretched

out, taking care to keep herself covered. "So if you would care to leave…"

Leaving was the last thing on his mind. The first had everything to do with how she looked sprawled out on the bed, but he shoved away the hot, racy thoughts. "I'm not going anywhere, Nina, because annoying as you are, you're my only lead."

"I told you, I know nothing."

"This was Terry's room."

"No."

Leaning forward, he took his gaze from her body and opened the chest. Like the vanity table, it was full. Reaching in, he pulled out a string with two tiny triangles of bright yellow attached to it. "What…"

"Bathing suit top."

He'd have used the term *top* loosely. The bottoms came next, also consisting mostly of string, with one tiny patch of material in the front. "Yours, I suppose," he said dryly, dangling it from his finger for Nina to inspect.

Her face went fiery red. "Um…yes, of course."

"Uh-huh."

"It is!"

"Prove it."

"H-how?"

"Put it on." At his wicked suggestion, she went even redder, and it was everything he could do not to laugh in her face.

"I will not."

"What a shame." Tossing it onto the bed, he went back to the chest. Out came a bright-yellow sundress that presumably covered up the bikini, though it was also majorly short on material.

Imagining the prim and reserved Nina in it did odd things to his head.

And his body.

Annoyed at the loss of concentration, Rick dived back into the chest and came up with a matching yellow beach bag. Inside was an empty gum wrapper, a tube of lipstick and a little orange pill.

Stumped, he stared down at the things. "Yours, too, right?"

"Of course."

He opened the lipstick. Cherry red. Slanting a doubtful look at Nina, he shook his head. "Try again."

"I wear lipstick."

"Not this color, you don't." Tossing it aside, he picked up the pill, which could be anything. "I can't imagine you on drugs, but since I've seen and heard everything in my day, try me. Go ahead,'' he said into her stubborn silence. ''Tell me it's yours.''

''I—'' She stared at the little pill and chewed her lip.

''Untangle yourself from that ridiculous blanket, it's not covering anything I haven't already seen anyway. Get out of the bed and come talk to me.''

Surprising him by doing exactly that, he watched as she rose out of the bed, tossed back her hair and stared at him regally. ''Okay. This is not my bedroom.''

''No,'' he said with feigned shock. ''Do tell.''

''You do not have to be rude about it. I decided I could tell you that much, at least. I have been trying to protect my sister's past.''

Since he'd screwed up protecting the one person who had ever really mattered to him, he found himself utterly unable to respond to that.

A first.

''My sister was a bit—'' eyes sad, voice quiet, she looked around the bedroom ''—flamboyant, I guess you would say. Wild. Loved the party life. But she was also much, much more than that. She was incredibly intelligent, and had an amazing business sense. She ran All That Glitters, you know.''

''No, I didn't.''

"She knew how to get the most of out that place, how to make it shine. While I—" she lifted a shoulder "—I am just a jewelry designer."

He doubted Nina Monteverde was "just" anything. "So now you run All That Glitters?"

"Yes."

"And the necklace Terry wore in that picture…was that your work?"

She nodded.

"You're good."

"It is my life," she said simply. "Terry's is the business end though, and I miss her with all my heart."

He had no idea why she was suddenly telling him all this. Either she'd finally come to the conclusion he wasn't going to hurt her, or maybe she just wanted him the hell out of here, and thought by giving him a few tidbits, he'd go.

No matter which, he was learning some interesting things. "You just talked about her in the present tense, Nina."

"Yes, I know." She met his gaze then, directly. "It is hard to let go, as I love—*loved*. See? I loved her very much."

Oh, she was good. "What happened?"

A little shrug and a big break in eye contact as she turned away. "All I can tell you is that she came to work one morning, like always, and was immediately arrested for embezzlement and smuggling gems, neither of which was true. She was framed. While awaiting trial, she jumped bail.''

''Then showed up dead.''

''Yes, after a boating accident off Galveston Island. She was sailing into an approaching storm, and drowned.''

''She died wanted for her crimes?''

''I tried to help, tried to find who framed her—and she was framed, believe me—but I could not, not by myself, and no one else could help.''

Again, that reference to being utterly alone. Rick didn't want to acknowledge she was as alone as he, didn't want to bond with her over that. ''But she was innocent.''

''Oh yes,'' she breathed, turning back, her entire heart in her eyes, so much that it hurt to look at her. ''She was most definitely innocent. My sister was a lot of things, but not a thief. Never.''

Rick withheld judgment. ''And your business didn't suffer from the scandal?''

''At first, yes. But eventually it died down.'' Her expression darkened as she once again looked at him. ''Until now, that is. With you digging everything up, who knows what will happen?''

Her indignation seemed as real as her grief, and gave him more than a moment's pause.

What was the real truth?

Could Terry Monteverde have faked her death, then disappeared to have the baby, only to later really die?

That would be a great coincidence, and Rick didn't believe in coincidences.

Still, that niggle of doubt bothered him, as did Nina's beautiful eyes and seeming sincerity.

He didn't want to trust her. Didn't want to trust anyone. So he held up the bathing suit, lipstick and pill one more time, forcing himself to remember that no matter how hauntingly beautiful, how vulnerable, this woman was capable of lying.

He needed to remember that. "So these were Terry's."

She bit her lower lip.

"Nina."

"No."

"No?"

"This was her bedroom, but we often shared clothes. As I told you, these things are mine."

NINA LIFTED her gaze to Rick's, forced herself to look right into his eyes, though it was one of the hardest things she'd ever done. But she'd do anything to protect the sister she loved with all her heart, anything, including facing down the toughest, most enigmatic man she'd ever met.

Not to mention the most gorgeous.

Reaching out, he once again twirled the thong bikini bottom around his finger, a wicked half smile twisting his lips. "Then, as I said, prove it."

Grabbing the bathing suit, she tossed it over her shoulder. "In your dreams."

"I have a feeling that could be arranged," he muttered, picking up the orange pill again. "We're back to this, then. What is it?"

"I cannot recall."

In response, he opened the adjoining door, which was a bathroom, and once again, as if she were no more potentially dangerous than a flea, turned his back on her.

If only she had the nerve to clobber him over his very handsome head! If only someone knew where she was, darn it.

John Henry knew, not that he'd care if she didn't show up at work. Maybe he'd mention it. Preferably to Meg Turner, the woman in bookkeeping. With the financials due tomorrow, she'd be wondering.

But would the standoffish Meg care if Nina

didn't show up? Probably not, as Meg had been hired by Terry, and seemed unhappy without her.

Nope, no one would notice.

Searching through the medicine cabinet, Rick suddenly went very still.

Behind him, staring at nothing but his wide shoulders so rippled with strength, Nina swallowed hard.

When he turned around, he was holding up a small bottle, mouth grim, eyes hard. "Yours, huh?"

Oops. This was bad, very bad. "Um—"

"Let me refresh your memory." He shook the bottle. "Seasickness pills. Still want to claim that little orange pill as yours?"

"Um—"

"Give it up, Nina. I know damn well you'd die before wearing that yellow scrap for a bathing suit. And don't even try to tell me you bought that sundress designed to give fully grown men heart failure. I won't buy that, and I won't buy you wearing screw-me-red lipstick, so I sure as hell won't buy this pill being yours."

She just stared at him, utterly unused to being so thoroughly cross-examined.

"I suppose you can tell me why Terry, a woman

prone to seasickness, would go out sailing in an approaching squall?''

He took a step toward her, and suddenly the rather spacious bathroom seemed far too confining for the both of them. She backed up and found herself caged in by the sink.

He kept coming, a strange light in his eyes. ''You're not talking.''

''I…'' He had the most amazing, arresting, mesmerizing eyes. She couldn't tear her gaze away, and yet she needed to duck, to run past him and go for the phone, for anything that would get her far, far away.

''You what?'' he asked softly, pinning her to the sink by placing a hand on either side of her hips. His mouth curved slightly. ''Run out of excuses? Lies? What?''

''I have nothing to say to you.''

''Wrong answer.''

''I have my own questions!'' She risked his wrath by lifting her hands and shoving against his chest.

She'd have had more luck trying to move a brick wall.

''Your own questions, huh?'' He cocked his head. ''Okay, that's fair. I've asked enough of my own. Go ahead—ask me a question.''

"Just one?"

He looked down at the hands that were still on his hard, unyielding chest.

She yanked them back.

"Just one," he said, lifting a mocking brow, entirely unmoved by her fear, by her frustration, by the fact she'd touched him.

Her hands were burning. "And you will answer?" she asked doubtfully, oddly breathless.

"You won't know until you try, will you?"

If only he'd back up. This close she could see his eyes were so green, so fathomless she could have drowned in them. There were fine lines fanning out from the corners, lines that she somehow doubted were from laughter. His hair curled around the collar of his shirt.

And his mouth, *Meu Deus,* what a mouth. "If you had found Terry here, would you have turned her in?"

He frowned. "To the law? No."

"But—"

He set a finger to her lips, a touch that electrified her from the inside out. "One question," he said in a voice of silk. "That was all I agreed to. Now *I* get one. Where is she?"

Nina stiffened, and would have backed up if she

could. Now was the time to run, she decided, and she ducked, intending to go for it.

He had her against the wall, held there by his body, before she could blink. "Going somewhere?"

Locking her jaw, she refused to talk.

"Lord, save me from stubborn women," he sighed, a motion that brought her body in even fuller contact with his long, lean, tough one. "Is this your decision then? Are you going to keep running without talking to me?"

She glared up at him.

"Okay, just remember, I tried to give you a way out of this." With that warning, he pulled something out of his back pocket.

She heard the click of metal, then another, and looked down in horror.

He'd handcuffed her to him.

CHAPTER FIVE

TOY CONNOISSEUR—and brilliant gem thief, if he did say so himself—Leo Hayes paced the length of his spacious living room, which overlooked the bay.

It was a gorgeous night. Brilliant stars made the water sparkle. During the day, the view became even more spectacular, because on the beach far below the cliffs where he'd had his mansion built lay wall-to-wall bathing beauties, all scantily dressed.

Leo had only dreamed of such a world, and now it was his.

He'd made his name by being the best toy maker in all of North America. And thanks to his contacts, he was well on his way in South America as well.

But that's not what had made him wealthy beyond reason. No, that came from his little hobby— smuggling gems.

And yet that lucrative sideline had been yanked

out from beneath his feet, all in one swipe, thanks to Terry Monteverde. She'd been framed for embezzling and gem smuggling, in supposed cahoots with his operation here in Rio, and his entire setup had been shut down.

By a stroke of luck—and some heavy bribing—Leo himself had only had one brush with the law. Regardless, he wanted his revenge, since Terry had ended up with two of his most precious diamonds, which had been stolen to implicate her.

They were still missing.

Oh, yes, he wanted his revenge, though fat lot of good that would do him now that she was dead.

He really resented that.

"It's a pretty evening, right, boss?"

Maybe. But he saw none of it, saw nothing but the three minions standing nervously before him, shifting uncomfortably on their feet at his unwavering stare.

"You've failed me," he said quietly.

They trembled.

"I asked for one thing. Watch the sister. Find out if she has my diamonds. How difficult could that be?"

"Senhorita Nina Monteverde has been watched very carefully," one dared to say, though his voice quavered. "We've not seen or heard of your diamonds."

Leo slid his hands into his pockets, filling his fingers with the two toy marbles he always kept there. The cool comfort of them rolling between his fingers soothed his temper. Slightly. "What *have* you seen?"

"The American bounty hunter. He's been sniffing around for a few days."

"Why?"

The three men shuffled some more and studied their shoes, the ceiling, anything but Leo, which only enraged him.

"You do not know," he breathed softly. "You should. It's what I pay you for."

"He's after Nina Monteverde." The one who spoke took a sharp look from Leo, and he ducked his head. "He followed her to the mountain estate…we think."

"You think." Leo nodded thoughtfully, worried the marbles between his fingers, and sighed. "You think. Obviously, you moron, someone *else* is searching for my diamonds."

Three faces looked dismayed. After all, the diamonds were an unusual, perfectly matched pair worth millions, and had last been seen in the possession of the dead Monteverde sister.

Now someone was following Nina.

"I should kill all of you," he said conversationally.

They looked horrified.

"But I will give you one more chance."

Three eager heads nodded with relief.

"Find out who the American is working for, and exactly what he wants. You do that, and I will forget how stupid you all are."

NINA REACHED for her glass of water, heard the clank of metal on metal, and glared at the man seated at the kitchen table with her, the man she was currently handcuffed to. Forcing her jaw to relax, she said, "I am thirsty."

"Are you?" Sprawled back in his chair, hands behind his head—which left her reaching up at a funny angle, not to mention sitting far too close to him—he crossed his booted feet as if he didn't have a care in the world.

While he appeared incredibly lax and maybe even lazy, Nina knew this to be far from true. Coiled in that stretched-out body was more muscle, more rangy strength than she'd ever seen in a man.

Granted, she had little experience. Okay, *one* experience. But that had been long ago. And no man she had ever met had been like Rick Singleton.

"Can you lean forward?" she asked frostily.

Only his eyes moved, and they landed on her with unerring accuracy. "I'm quite comfortable."

"But I want my water."

"All you have to do is talk to me. Tell me what I want to know."

"And you will let me go?"

"I told you I would."

She thought about Terry, about how much danger her sister must be in that she hadn't been able to contact Baba to let her know she was okay.

If she was okay.

At that thought, Nina's eyes burned. Her throat closed as the grief welled up and grabbed her by the heart.

Please, Terry, please be okay.

With a soft oath, Rick lifted his feet off the table, setting his chair back down. "Here." He shoved the cup of water beneath her nose. "Drink."

She sniffed and shook her head.

"Damn it, not again. Drink."

"No."

"You just said you were thirsty, and now you're not? Women!"

"This has nothing to do with my being female."

"Then what's your problem?"

"What is my problem! I worked sixty hours this

week, and now it is the middle of the night and I am so tired I can hardly see straight. Oh, and yes, I am handcuffed to a kidnapper."

"I am *not* a kidnapper."

He looked genuinely horrified, which made her let out a short laugh. "Right. A terrorist, then. I am handcuffed to a terrorist. My apologies."

"And I'm not a terrorist!"

"Then let me go."

"Tell me where Terry is."

"So you can terrorize her for the jewels you think she embezzled? She is dead! *Dead,* I told you." Her voice cracked on that last word and she shut her mouth. Then she let out a long breath, her shoulders sagging as exhaustion came on like a freight train. She looked at her feet, her bare toes void of toenail polish and toe rings—as Terry's would not have been. "And I feel very alone, if you want the truth. Alone and…" She wouldn't say frightened, she wouldn't admit that much.

Slowly he uncoiled and came to his full height, forcing her to stand, as well. Slowly he looked her up and then down, reminding her that she was not dressed, not even close.

Her nipples hardened, though she wasn't cold. She crossed her arms over her chest, but he'd noticed, he'd definitely noticed, and something in his eyes shifted, warmed. Even his voice sounded husky. "I'm not a kidnapper, and definitely not a terrorist," he said in a tone that made her knees wobbly. "I'm not a stranger, either. I introduced myself."

Standing so close to him, so close she could see the light reflecting in the depths of his spectacular green eyes, could see his long, dark lashes and a small but jagged scar over one brow, she felt an odd unfurling in her belly. A heat.

She should step back, *wanted* to step back, but was unwilling to let him see he could wrangle a reaction from her.

Even if she didn't understand that reaction.

It was the oddest thing—she was quite literally bound to him, but she felt…free. It had been so long, so very long, since she'd been able to let herself go, to react as she wanted.

Actually, she'd *never* let herself go. Had never let herself react, except in a way that had been completely acceptable to her family.

A little stunned at the realization, she stared at him.

Frowning, he lifted their joined hands, clearly misinterpreting her expression. "I would let you go for the truth. It's important."

"I should tell you everything I know, while you

tell me exactly nothing.'' It felt good to say what was on her mind, to not hold back. ''That is fair, right?''

He was not nearly as pleased with her ''freedom'' as she was. ''Are you twisting this all around on purpose? I told you I wouldn't hurt you. And I wouldn't hurt your sister.''

''No, actually you never did tell me that last part.''

He stared at her for a long moment. ''I beg your pardon. Let me tell you now. I would never hurt your sister. Are you admitting she's alive?''

He'd very nearly caught her, hadn't he? He was very, very good.

She would have to be better. ''I am admitting nothing. And neither have you.''

He inhaled deeply, then slowly let out his breath. ''Okay. Fine. You win. The man who hired me to find Terry, he's the man in the picture I showed you.'' He took the Polaroid out of his pocket with his free hand and held it out.

She grabbed it, looked down at it into her sister's happy face and felt her heart crack. ''This is at Carnival.''

''Yes, a year and a half ago.''

''I was in London.''

''And she was with him.''

"She did not have a boyfriend, she never did. She enjoyed men, too much to stick with just one."

"They were lovers."

"Only for one night then."

"Yes," he agreed. "Only for the one night. He woke up and she was gone, without even sharing her name. 'It's all in the eyes' was all she'd told him when he asked."

"Terry truly believed the eyes were mirrors to the soul."

Rick rewarded her with a smile that quite simply stole her breath. *Meu Deus,* but she hoped he didn't use that weapon often.

He looked at the picture again. "Mitch went back to the States the next day, but he's never forgotten your sister. Things were busy in his life and work for a while and he was injured on the job. But now he's free, and he wants to find her."

He wasn't looking at her, and she knew there was more, much more. "To sleep with her again?" she asked.

"I think he wants more than that." He met her gaze then. "It seems very important to him."

Could he be distracting her with sentiment to get information?

Would he?

His eyes were deep and full of mysteries. His

face blank. He was a ruthless, dangerous man, not to be trusted. She looked at the picture again, too. Terry and the man were gazing into each other's eyes with more than just the lust of the Carnival and good drink. There was affection with all that heat, and seeing it, when Terry hadn't been overly fond of sharing her heart, made Nina want to believe.

It would feel good to have an ally in this terror, but to admit that seemed weak.

Yet even more disturbing was the fact that while she was truly terrified for Terry, she was not terrified for herself. Even shackled to this man and half-naked, she wasn't afraid of him.

How horribly revealing.

"What?" he asked quietly, tipping up her chin with his thumb when she wouldn't look at him. "What are you thinking?"

That he was devastatingly sexy. And that she couldn't, shouldn't be having such thoughts about a man who'd stop at nothing to get what he wanted.

She shouldn't be having those thoughts period! She was not a woman prone to such things as—as heat and need and lust. She never had been. "Nothing."

"Oh, I think it is something."

She had to smile at his formal speech. He was mocking her again. "Now you are a mind reader?"

"I'm a bounty hunter, same thing."

"Have you always hunted people for a living?"

"Have you always so neatly avoided talking about yourself?"

"It is a skill."

"See?" He shook his head. "You're good. Very good. Was your sister as good as you?"

"Not nearly, but only because she *liked* to talk about herself." Nina found herself smiling with fond memories. "Her zest for life and her way with the business were legendary. Everyone at All That Glitters misses her. I miss her." Sadness crept back. "All those hopes and dreams of hers, left unfulfilled."

"What about your hopes and dreams?"

Nina looked up at him, startled. "What?"

He leaned even closer, the sound of metal on metal reminding her they were still joined.

She'd actually nearly forgotten.

He lifted his free hand and tucked a loose strand of hair behind her ear. The touch of his finger on her skin sent a shiver racing down her spine.

"All you talk about is Terry," he said. "Her life, her dreams."

"They were important."

"Yes. But what about *your* life? *Your* dreams? Surely you have some for yourself other than living in the shadow of your sister."

No one—not her father, not her own sister, not a single friend—had ever asked Nina about her hopes and dreams, not once.

That this man, a perfect stranger, a professional bounty hunter to whom she meant nothing more than a means to his paycheck, would ask... It stunned her.

He stunned her.

"What floats your boat, Nina? What is it that makes you want to get up in the morning?"

"Why are you asking?"

"Because we're here." He lifted their joined hands. "Stuck together—"

"Your own doing."

"—and if you don't feel like telling me what I want to know, I might as well learn about you. What's your passion?"

Certain she couldn't have heard right, she gaped at him.

"And don't tell me you don't have one, I won't believe you."

"Why not?"

"Because you're a very passionate woman."

That he thought so was a ridiculous compliment.

But he was greatly mistaken.

And still waiting for her to answer him.

"My passion?" She lifted her shoulders. "I suppose designing jewelry."

"And you're good at it."

She used to be, before the added burden of the business side of All That Glitters. "I could be better, if—"

"Nope." He wagged a finger in her face. "Now, see, right there is where you went wrong."

"Excuse me?"

"There shouldn't be any ifs. Not with hopes and dreams. There should only be when."

"Yes, you are right. But—" But she'd been too worried about her sister to be good at anything in a long time. "What about you?"

His eyes shuttered. "This isn't about me."

No, it wasn't, though suddenly she wanted it to be. If only things were different, if only she could trust this man to help her….

Could she?

And wasn't that just the problem.

She was too afraid to take the chance.

CHAPTER SIX

THE HANGING CLOCK on the wall of the living room chimed twice.

Two in the morning.

Rick had gone much longer without sleep. Hell, he'd gone days while on a case, but he doubted Nina had. There were delicate purple splotches beneath her eyes, and she looked dead on her feet.

He shoved the unwanted sympathy right out of his head. He didn't care if she was tired, he wasn't here to baby-sit.

He needed answers. And the deeper he got, the more he learned about the reckless, eccentric Terry and the willowy, softer Nina, the more he wanted those answers.

That bothered him.

"Okay, here's the deal," he told a nodding off Nina, deciding to play hardball so that she'd co-operate and he could get the hell on with it. "You know I'm not going anywhere until I learn where Terry is."

She rolled her eyes upward. "Terry is—"

"Dead, yes. But since you won't look me in the eyes when you say it, you'll excuse me for not believing you."

Her eyes sparked but she didn't say another word.

"Fine. Be stubborn." Purposely, he wiggled the handcuffs, not enjoying her look of unease as much as he'd have thought. "I have all night."

"The night is nearly over."

"Which reminds me…" He sat on the couch— a pleasingly long, wide one—and jerked just hard enough on the handcuffs that she was forced to sit next to him. "I'm tired."

Nina's eyes widened. "You are *not* going to sleep."

"That is exactly what I plan on doing." He lifted his hands to the buttons on his shirt.

She let out a squeak and tugged on his manacled hand. "What are you doing?"

He continued unbuttoning his shirt with his free hand, though he had to admit, he'd enjoyed it more with her fingers brushing his chest. He shrugged out of the garment, letting it hang on the handcuffs still hampering them both.

She stared at his bared chest and shoulders, mouth hanging open just a little, and the sight of her speechless over his body did something to his gut.

Okay, not his gut.

The area due *south* of his gut.

Her eyes all but devoured him, and he couldn't believe how arousing that was. What was with him? He'd been wanted by a woman before, more times than he could remember. He knew he had a shape that pleased the opposite sex, and normally he wasn't above using that to his advantage.

But not here, not with this woman who looked as if maybe she was far more innocent than he could imagine. It wasn't his thing, playing with a woman who believed in love and hearts and roses and happily ever after.

Damn it, all he'd wanted was to intimidate her into speaking. "You're staring," he said unkindly.

"Because you are not wearing a shirt."

"That's what happens when one removes it," he agreed. "They become shirtless."

"It is inappropriate."

He had to laugh. God, she was so formal. And so shockingly, madly, wildly sexy—without even knowing it. "I hate sleeping in clothes."

She made a strangled sound, then pointed to his pants. "Those are staying on."

"You say such sexy things, Nina. You'd better watch it, or I'll get the wrong idea."

It took her a moment to realize he was kidding, and her frown deepened.

She didn't take her eyes off him.

He realized how aware of her he suddenly was. How he noticed the slight flare in her gaze, and the way she nervously licked her lips. How her hands fisted, as if she were having trouble keeping them to herself.

It wasn't often he let himself fantasize. Mostly he needed his mind sharp and focused. But he was fantasizing now, in a big way, and it was definitely hampering his thinking.

He scooted farther down the couch, trying to get comfortable, trying to shut her out of his mind— yeah, right!—and sighed with pleasure at the soft, cozy cushions. He closed his eyes, considering himself lucky. He'd slept in some real sleaze buckets while on previous cases. "Maybe when I wake up, you'll feel more like sharing info about your sister and her whereabouts."

"I told you all I know."

"I doubt that."

"You are really not leaving until…?"

"Not until."

"But—"

Opening his eyes, he waited with a raised brow, but she only glared at him. Shrugging, he kicked off his shoes and lay back, stuffing a throw pillow beneath his head. When he put up his feet, Nina let out a disbelieving huff. He smiled as he stretched out, eyes closed, knowing she was sitting stiffly at his hip, attempting to not touch him any more than absolutely necessary.

A long moment passed, during which he imagined her watching him breathe.

And even that simple action became difficult.

He wondered if she'd noticed his erection straining at the fly of his pants, or how he'd fisted his hands with the tension coursing through him.

"Rick." The word was choked out, and when he looked at her, she was blushing.

Yeah, she'd noticed.

Only it wasn't flattery he saw in those dark, dark eyes so solemnly watching him, but…fear?

Well, hell. "Oh, lie down," he said far more gruffly than he'd intended.

"But—"

"Lie down."

She held herself rigidly at his side, her bare thigh brushing his bare side. He could feel her warmth, the soft creaminess of her skin, and was already cursing himself for a fool.

"It is not that easy, you—you Neanderthal!" she snapped. "Maybe *you* are used to being handcuffed to different people every night, maybe you even like it, but for me...this is difficult to say the least."

Lord, she was going to talk all night, and if he didn't shut his eyes and put himself into dreamland, he was going to have a hell of a time here. His body was already nearly shaking with the sexual tension holding him captive, and he didn't like it. "First of all," he said, "if you mean using whatever tactic at my disposal to get the job done, then fine, I'm a Neanderthal."

"This—" she held up their joined hands "—is illegal."

"Give me a break, we're in Brazil. Country of sinners."

"*Let...me...go.* I want—"

"Look, unless you're going to tell me where your sister is, how about you don't talk?"

She opened her mouth to retort to that—hotly, he was quite certain—so he put a finger to her soft lips, nearly groaning at the feel of her. He thought of all the uses he could find for that mouth and then *did* groan, his hips actually arching of their own accord. "I mean it, Nina."

Her gaze jerked up to his. "You are..." Her

face went even redder as she resolutely stared at him. "You know."

"Sporting a hard-on? Yes. Why, yes, I am."

Her gaze again darted down his body, past his chest, right to the point of impact.

He got even harder. "Okay, this is how this is going to work. Lie down. Close your eyes. And shut up."

He himself did all three, and waited with bated breath, silently begging her to do the same.

But even he had to admit, if the situation was reversed, he'd have a hell of a time doing as he'd ordered her.

"You will not...touch me?"

"Believe me," he said, eyes still closed. "Sleep is all I'm after." *Liar, liar, pants on fire.*

"I wish I knew you," she whispered.

"You know what you need to. I told you I wouldn't hurt you."

"Actually, I believe that part," she said, surprising him into opening his eyes. "What I want to believe is that you are an honorable man. That you are a man who would not...take advantage of a woman like me."

"A woman like you?"

She blushed again, but kept her eyes on his. "Inexperienced."

Aw, hell, he didn't want to know this. Didn't want her looking at him as if maybe he could be someone he wasn't.

Couldn't she see he was a man for hire, and nothing more?

That he would never, ever again get personally involved in a case? That he'd never let anyone touch him on the inside, because his emotions were gone? He'd buried them good and deep when Mary Jo had died, so much so that he'd been certain they no longer even existed.

Until tonight.

Normally, being with a woman for longer than it took to mutually satisfy each other made him claustrophobic. But perversely, the more time he spent with Nina, the less he could seem to resist her charms. Truth was, since he first saw her, he'd been tempted to turn his bounty hunter skills on himself and find the real Rick.

And then share that man with her.

"Lie down," he said, feeling strained. "I can behave myself."

"Take off the handcuffs. Please?"

"And have you take off again? I don't think so. Now hurry up. I'm tired."

She hesitated another very long, painful moment. Finally, she tugged at the hem of her T-shirt and, careful to keep herself covered, gingerly lay on her back next to him, their joined hands between them.

The silence stretched out.

Nina's feet rubbed together, so did her thighs. Her nipples, abraded by the material of her shirt, stood at erect attention.

And he couldn't take his eyes off her.

Then she shivered.

With a particularly foul oath, Rick grabbed the blanket off the back of the couch and tossed it over them, hoping against hope that if he couldn't actually *see* her incredible body, he might be able to forget it.

Didn't happen.

In strained silence, they lay there in the dark, both holding their breath.

It was a long, long time before Nina finally dozed off.

And an even longer time for Rick.

THE DOUBT that had taken root deep inside couldn't be assuaged.

Terry Monteverde was dead.

Yes. She was. Dead.

Dead.

Repeating it became as necessary as breathing.

Terry Monteverde was dead. Dead. Dead. It didn't help that the body had never been viewed.

Damn it, why had that been?

And why hadn't the thought occurred before now?

Because a coffin was a coffin, and when you saw it being lowered into the ground, you believed it to be full, that's why.

There would be no peace, no relief of this tension, until the coffin had been opened and the body of Terry Monteverde seen. Now.

It was midnight.

In the cemetery.

The stuff nightmares were made of. But that fit. This life had indeed become a nightmare, and the irony of the entire situation did not fail to hit as the dirt and twigs crunched beneath booted feet.

The walk was long, but the moon was high. Far below, the city of Rio glittered.

And fed a growing, crawling, frustrated temper.

That this could happen now, a year and a half later, was beyond imagination. That Terry Monteverde could possibly be alive, walking around with all her wild beauty, stoked an uncontrollable rage.

The graveyard, on a steep, mostly overgrown hill, caused much cursing and slipping and sliding.

And more cursing.

Finally, the right grave…just ahead. She's dead. Dead!

She had to be.

By moonlight and flashlight, the engraved name shimmered in the night.

Senhorita Terry Monteverde.

She was right there, long gone and buried.

She was.

"You got what you deserved, Terry Monteverde!"

Still, the niggle of doubt wouldn't go away. It had grown steadily over the past weeks, even more with that American bounty hunter dogging Nina's heels the past few days. It made no sense; Nina was a nobody. Something was up, something was wrong, and it had led to this midnight run of the graves.

Luckily, there was no concrete vault, and the dirt was soft and giving beneath the shovel, and within moments, a good hole was started. The rest took longer than expected. Hours actually, and by the time the coffin was exposed, breathing had become ragged, the lines between nightmare and reality blurred.

"You are dead. You are!"

Looking at the coffin wasn't enough. It had to

be opened, which was shockingly easy. Jumping down into the hole, covered in dirt by this time and no longer even caring, opening the lid with shaking hands...

A scream pierced the night. "No, no, no, no, no!" With another horrible cry, knees hit the dirt. Fists slammed on the wood.

There was no body inside the coffin.

Only sandbags.

A dirt-streaked face was raised to the night sky. "Revenge!" This was a solemn vow. "I will get revenge, Terry Monteverde! I will find you and make you wish you had died in that boat!"

IN HER DREAMS, Nina was cold and afraid.

Alone.

Shivering, she tried to escape by turning away, found there was indeed warmth to be had, if she wanted it. All she had to do was roll from her back to her side and there it was.

All she'd ever wanted, within her reach.

Going for that incredible heat, she snuggled in, feeling it surround her, sighing with pleasure, and something even more.

Sleeping had never felt so good.

There came a low rumble in her ear, a cross between an encouraging groan and a growl, and with that sound an incredibly warm, strong arm slipped around her waist. A hand nudged the small of her back, urging her even closer.

She felt safe and secure, and because this was a dream—a really great dream—she sighed again and practically crawled up that delicious hard length.

It felt heavenly.

Smelled heavenly, too, sort of like a warm, toasty, sleepy male, but that couldn't be right since she rarely had erotic dreams.

But it felt so real.

She couldn't hold herself back, she had to press her face into his throat and inhale deeply, she had to touch, so she lifted a hand to do just that, anticipating the feel of smooth, hot flesh, but her hand was caught—

On handcuffs.

Jerked awake by the horrible reality of her life—being manacled to an American bounty hunter with a sharp mouth and an even sharper desire to get the truth from her—she went stock-still and opened her eyes.

Skin.

That was all she saw.

She was face-to-face, chest to chest, thigh to

thigh with a very warm body, looking at a throat…
Rick's throat.

She'd crawled all over him!

He wasn't moving though, which was strange,
so she tipped her head back very slowly, very carefully, as if she'd found herself in the path of a
cougar, which of course she had.

The cougar had the nerve to still be asleep.

If she'd been a mean-spirited woman, she might
have smacked him, but the fact was, *she'd* curled
into *him,* and *she'd* pressed her body full length to
his, while he'd done just as he'd promised.

He'd slept.

The sun was peeking over the horizon, and she
could feel the rays slowly climbing through the
room and heating it up.

It would be a warm one today, even up here in
the mountains.

Such banal thoughts momentarily took her away
from the fact she'd wrapped herself around this
perplexing—albeit gorgeous—man, but not for
long, not when every pulse point drummed furi-
ously, not when she felt all liquidy and hot, yet
cold as ice all at the same time.

She was deadly certain she knew what was
wrong with her, and the knowing was not com-
forting.

She was lusting.

Lusting!

After a man holding her against her will, a man she had no idea if she could trust with her secrets, a man who somehow both drew and repelled her.

Okay, that was a lie.

He didn't repel her, not even close.

The way they were lying, she could see only his face. To tip her head down any further would surely wake him up, but she didn't need to see the rest, not when she could feel perfectly well, and oh my, what she felt. His one free hand was curled around her waist, the weight of his arm over her hip. He had one leg between hers, and Nina was shocked to find her own thigh muscles tensed, holding him there, as if she had been afraid he'd move that leg away.

Good thing he was fast asleep, God only knew what he'd think of the way she'd plastered herself to him.

But how to back off now without waking him?

Slowly, very slowly, she relaxed her leg muscles, which were sore, as if she'd clung to him all night. Her face flamed at the thought.

Nina Monteverde never clung!

Okay, now…she eased her legs back carefully.

"Mmm," he said, his eyes still closed, his far

too sexy mouth curved ever so slightly. His hand, low on her back, tightened, his fingers playing softly over her bare skin.

Her bare skin!

One glance downward assured her that yes, oh yes, her worse nightmare had occurred. The hem of her shirt had risen to her waist, and he indeed had his hand against her spine, just above her panties.

"Mmm," he said again, those fingers of his dancing across her now goose-bumped flesh. His mouth, only inches from hers, dipped to her throat. His chest, bare and warm, pressed against hers, while his hips arched just enough that she could feel every inch of him.

He was fully aroused, just as he'd been last night.

"Rick," she said, meaning to sound strong and certain, but really sounding as breathless as if she'd run a marathon. "I think maybe we need to get up."

She thought maybe they needed to get up?

That was a laugh! She needed to run far and fast. She needed a cold shower. She needed a reality check of some kind, and she was smart enough to know they needed to move, before this strange sense of yearning and aching went any further, before he—

Oh, God.

Before he did that, exactly that! His mouth opened on her neck in a hot, wet kiss, making her want to purr and stretch like a kitten.

His thigh once again slipped between hers, gliding high enough to stroke her oh-so-sensitized flesh in such a way that she actually cried out.

At the sound, he went utterly still for the longest moment in history, before slowly lifting his head to stare down into her face.

That was all he moved, just his head, so that they were still entwined, but the look on his face, such perfect befuddlement and arousal and heat and frustration, made her let out a high laugh. "I, um, think we shifted somewhat in our sleep."

He didn't answer, just looked at her, his entire body tense.

"I was just going to get up." She bit her lip. "But you would have to move, too, you see, and I was not sure how to wake you."

Why wasn't he saying anything?

And why, oh why, when she was with him, did she want to throw out the good girl image she'd so carefully cultivated all her life and be the real Nina? "Rick?"

He leaned toward her.

Or maybe she leaned toward him.

She managed a little smile. "I think—"

"You think too much." His voice was low and husky from sleep.

She closed her eyes in the echo of that husky voice. It was a strong sound, and a very sexy one. "Yes, but—"

"You talk too much, too." He leaned over her, his shoulders blocking out the morning sun, the morning heat, everything but him, and when her body arched up, just a little, he moaned.

"Okay, maybe I do think and talk too much," she whispered. "But—"

"Nina." That was it, just her name, in that serrated voice that told her he was doing the same slow burn that she was.

Her body was fitting itself more tightly to his in order to try to quench that burn, and he met her more than halfway.

"Rick, I—"

In answer, his mouth covered hers, swallowing anything she might have managed to eke out. It was a fierce kiss, with little to temper it, and she fed the heat by opening her mouth to his. Both of them lifted their hands toward each other at the same time, and both came up against the restraints of the handcuffs.

Catching her face with his free hand, Rick brought her mouth back to his, using his tongue to bind her to him while he entwined the fingers of their connected hands. The gesture was so unexpectedly sweet, it threw Nina off. Fierceness she could have resisted. Roughness she could have resisted.

Anything but this tenderness and raw, desperate hunger that went on and on. When he finally pulled back, she could only blink up at him. "That was..." Simply the most soul-searching, heartwrenching kiss of her life.

"Yeah." He didn't looked pleased.

She licked her lips, unable to believe how much she wanted, ached, needed. This had never happened to her, never, and she had to have more to see if it could happen again. To see if it could get even better, though she couldn't imagine it. "Maybe we could try that just one more time, just to see if..."

He let out a short laugh, but in his eyes was a grim determination that scared her.

He'd already pulled away.

He was going to get up, wasn't going to give her one more kiss to treasure.

How could this have happened? How could she find herself attracted to the most ill-mannered, bad-tempered, dangerous, sexy man she'd ever met?

Okay, the attraction she understood. It wasn't her fault, or even his, it was simply chemical.

But there was more. He made her yearn for everything that had been missing in her life. For a moment she imagined how this would be if they actually liked each other, if they lived in a different place and time where they could trust each other. But those thoughts terrified her. He made her wonder about things better left alone, such as what it would be like to be made love to by such an intense, driven man.

"Please," she whispered, horrifying herself with the plea. "One more."

"Nina." There was a warning in his voice. A warning, and a plea as well.

He wasn't going to do it.

So for once in her life, she made the first move. She fisted her free hand in his hair, pulled his head to hers and planted her mouth on his.

CHAPTER SEVEN

ONE OF RICK'S favorite qualities in a woman was sexual aggression. He appreciated someone who knew what she wanted and wasn't shy about getting it, but in his head, Nina wasn't one of those women. She was sweet and refined and didn't have a horny bone in her body.

Not a woman for him, in other words.

But his body wasn't getting the message, not faced with her fumbling determination and that hot little bod arching closer to his. With the shirt twisted around her waist, he got another good long look at those nice white panties, and all the treasures they barely covered. "Nina—" His mouth watered. "Wait—"

"Shh. You talk too much," she said, throwing his words back in his face.

"Very funny. But you've got to hold on—"

"No." In her hurry to kiss him, she bumped her nose to his. She ground her tooth into his bottom lip. She slanted her head all wrong.

Then whimpered in frustration.

At the sound, at her obvious—but arousing as hell—attempts to attack him, something happened. Some sort of gentleness came over him that he never ordinarily felt.

And that devastated him, because damn it, he was *feeling,* and he didn't want to! Warning bells started blaring—a little damn late now.

Still making those incredibly erotic, needy sounds in her throat, Nina once again crawled up his body, practically straddling him, her hips thrusting against his, which nearly, very nearly, made his entire body her slave forever. He quivered, and then, when she slid the neediest part of her over the neediest part of him, the quiver turned to a full body shudder. "Nina—"

She simply pressed her mouth harder to his, then reached up, probably to fist her other hand in his hair—and cried out.

The handcuffs, he thought with a vicious oath. And now she'd hurt herself, damn it. "Let me—"

She didn't slow down, she was still coming at him with that mouth that was going to headline his fantasies for many nights to come. "Nina. Stop." He reached for her wrist, but she pulled it away, shaking her head, going for yet another kiss and missing, planting her mouth on the side of his. Her breasts were smashed against his chest, the thin T-shirt she wore no protection at all. The touch of her nipples against his skin made him groan, but still he tried to shake it off. "Let me see your wrist—"

"I'm fine!"

She was more than fine. Rumpled, sleepy-eyed, lips wet and full from his mouth, she looked incredible.

And vulnerable.

Hell. He wanted her.

Yet she was holding back on him in a big way. She'd lied about Terry, and anyone who'd lied couldn't be trusted. Hell, in his life, *no one* could be trusted.

Period.

He needed to remember that, no matter how sweet her warm, lush body felt against his. Pushing her away, he sat up. "So much for you being worried about me taking advantage."

She blushed, but didn't say a word.

Reaching into his pocket, he pulled out a small key. Grabbing her arm, holding it still, he unlocked the cuffs and let them fall.

When she would have tugged free, he held on, turned her hand over, palm up. Across the inside of her wrist was a nasty-looking bruise.

Guilt twisted inside him, and he ran a gentle finger over the swelling. *I'm sorry* seemed stupid and pathetic, not to mention most likely entirely unwelcome, since he'd been the one to purposely lock them together.

He hadn't been sorry when he'd done it, not when her eyes had flashed both heat and hatred. He certainly hadn't been sorry when they'd woken up wrapped tighter than a pretzel. Hell, he could still feel her nice, curvy body against his.

And that kiss...his body was still humming. Nope, he hadn't been sorry then either, wasn't capable of being sorry because his every brain cell had been on full lust alert.

But he was sorry now.

And judging by the look on her face, she knew it too. "If you tell me you regret that you kissed me—"

"Whoa," he said. "*You* kissed *me*."

"I kissed you back, but you kissed me first."

"Because I woke up with you all over me like bees on honey. Remember that part?"

"Rick..." She let out a breath and lifted her hands. "What are we doing?"

"I don't know about you. Me, I'm finding Terry."

"Because Mitch wants her."

"Yes."

"But why?"

He looked into her earnest face and knew this was the time to tell her about the baby.

But trusting her, when she so clearly had not trusted him, went deeply against the grain. And it left him feeling like an even bigger jerk, because now that he knew her a little bit, he knew exactly how much she'd welcome the news of Terry's baby.

"Rick?"

He'd tell her all when she told him all, and not a second before, and he'd just have to live with the guilt. "Maybe she was a good lay," he said cavalierly, and bingo, temper flashed hard and fast in her eyes.

"I see." Surging to her feet, she rubbed her wrist one more time, then turned away.

"Where are you going?"

"Why?" She stopped and looked at him over her shoulder. The very early morning sun glared in the windows, casting her beautifully glowing skin in a myriad of golds, and rendering her T-shirt absolutely sheer.

How many gorgeous women had he laid eyes on over the years? Plenty.

How many of those gorgeous women had made him hard enough to hammer nails? Plenty.

But how many of those gorgeous women made him want to drop to his knees and beg for forgiveness?

None.

"You going to handcuff me again if I do not tell you?" she asked.

"Just answer my question. Where are you going?"

"Back to Rio. I have work."

"What about the car I saw following you up here last night?"

"You are the only one who followed me."

"You don't know that."

Another shrug. "I know of no one who would care where I go or what I do. And as I have told you all I can about Terry, I no longer matter to you. Right?"

She was fishing, looking at him with a sort of half hope that made him hurt.

Did she want him to deny it? He couldn't. And since he hated to hurt, he purposely, carefully shut that look out. "Right."

The light in her eyes died, and he told himself he was glad, very glad.

And then she was gone, sequestered in her room, the lock firmly in place.

He got the message. *Stay out.*

Five minutes later she came back into the living room fully dressed in her Senhorita Nina Monteverde attire, hair firmly back, distant smile in place.

"You are still here," she said coolly.

"I thought I would follow you back into Rio."

"Sure. I would not want you to get lost."

"I'm not in danger of getting lost," he said through his teeth. "I—" What? Wanted to make sure she was safe?

He wasn't protecting her!

Not like he'd been honor bound to protect Mary Jo. But damn it, that didn't stop him from struggling uselessly against the need to see this woman safe.

"Do as you please," she said, lifting her bag to her shoulder. "I am leaving."

His gaze narrowed in on what stuck out of her bag, and he stepped close, putting his hand on her arm.

Impatience shimmered from her. "I am in a hurry."

"I can see that." He fingered past a file labeled "Financials" to the top of the yearbook she'd crammed in with her stuff. "Why are you taking this?"

"The financials are due today."

"The yearbook, Nina."

"No reason."

"Nina."

"Because I want to look at her again, all right?"

She was dead serious and in danger of crying. "All right."

"Now either handcuff me again, or let me go."

Tempting as the first thought was, he let her go.

But since she hadn't yet told him all she knew, he followed her, because the truth was out there, and he was convinced Nina had it.

HOW DARE HE kiss her as if she were the most important woman in the entire world, and then, when they were no longer so close she couldn't tell whose heartbeat was whose, look at her with those shuttered, cool eyes and act as if nothing had happened!

Something *had* happened, and Nina wasn't likely to forget it.

It was a known fact that one could not drive through the glorious mountains in Brazil and remain furious, even when one had finally been coaxed into trusting, where one hadn't trusted before.

The views were too stunning, too breathtaking for that.

She'd known, hadn't she? Known Rick Singleton was trouble. She'd known to never trust a man with eyes so green and deep and full of secrets.

But while in his arms, so safe and secure, she'd forgotten.

She did her best to hold on to her foul mood, but the high coastal peaks, so wild and lush and green, did their job on her temper. So did the pure azure sky, without a single cloud marring its beauty.

Then her cell phone rang, jarring her. "Hello?"

"It's Meg. You coming in today?"

Meg Turner had been Terry's pity hire, or so Terry had claimed privately to Nina. And since Meg had followed Terry from their college days together at Northwestern, desperately in need of a job, Nina had gone along with it.

It had worked out, mostly because Meg was a quiet, dedicated worker who so rarely made a mistake that they all joked she was half human and half computer. Meg never bothered with Nina, never joked around, never started a conversation, and never came to her with anything, even work, so Nina wondered at the odd phone call. "I will be there in a little while," she said slowly. "What is the matter?"

"Nothing…just wondering where you were. I'll see you in a little while then."

She clicked off before Nina could respond, leaving her to shrug and set the phone back down. She didn't have time to worry about Meg. Or about John Henry's attitude. Or how her father expected her to oversee all the business dealings when her heart had been given to the designing that she no longer had time for.

Because the sun was sharp, and the narrow, winding roads filled with crazy Brazilian drivers, Nina cranked up the music and forced her mind blank.

It worked for nearly the entire three-hour drive, until the very end, when in her rearview mirror, she caught sight of a motorcycle far back in her lane.

Apparently it wasn't enough to humiliate her in her mountain retreat—Rick had to follow her home to further the experience.

If he could catch her, that is. She was a native, and knew the roads intimately. She couldn't imagine how long he'd been in Rio, or really why he'd even landed there in the first place, but she ruthlessly used her advantage, randomly turning here and there, wherever she could, just to throw him off.

Once in the city, she really got into the game, going through as many neighborhoods as she could, even several *favelas,* changing her direction at will, so that surely the irritating American who kissed like heaven and looked like sin was good and lost.

Satisfaction coursed through her at that, childish as it was, but it lasted all the way home and up the walk of her condo.

All the way, in fact, to the front door.

Which was ajar.

She hadn't left her place unlocked, she knew it. But Terry had always made herself at home here, and with a surge of joy and hope, Nina charged in, expecting to find her sister sprawled out on the couch, drinking all Nina's soft drinks and watching the television, as if nothing had ever happened, as if they hadn't been separated by terrible circumstance for a year and a half.

That's not what Nina found, not at all, and it took a moment for the ransacked state of her condo to sink in.

Her couches were turned over, the lining cut open and stuffing pulled out. Bookshelves had been emptied to the floor, as well as her hutch. Glass and broken treasures and books and pictures...everything lay on the floor in a broken, crumpled heap.

And she'd charged in without thinking, even now standing out in the open, both her jaw and her heart on the floor as well.

They could still be here.

Quickly, she took a step backward, then another. And then, when no one reached out to grab her, whirled for the door.

And plowed into a solid wall with arms that reached up and hauled her close.

She fought like a madwoman, but it was all too much for her overtaxed brain; first the mad dash to Arraial do Cabo, then being frightened half to death by Rick, being held by him all night, then her flight back here. If she'd had time, she might have broken down, but somewhere over the past day she'd found an inner strength, a place in her brain where breaking down was not an option. She wasn't going down without a fight, no way, and she kicked out hard, connecting with a shin.

"It's me, damn it!"

Rick. *"Meu Deus!"* she whispered, sagging as adrenaline continued to course through her. "Someone—"

"Out," he said, still gripping her arms. "Get out and call the police."

She just looked at him blankly.

"Chame a polícia," he demanded, switching to her native Portuguese to reach her. *"Now."* He shoved her toward the door, and when he turned back to her living room, he was in full bounty hunter mode, all tough body stance, intense concentration on his face.

He had a gun in his hands.

She'd think about that later, she told herself, whipping out her cell phone, hitting her preprogrammed number for the police. Shaking, she brought the phone up to her ear and waited.

And waited.

Finally, a very long, tense moment later, she got through and gave her information, but all she could think was that she could no longer see Rick in the doorway. There was nothing, no sound, and she moved closer, trying to peek in.

She had one foot on the entry, one hand on the doorjamb, craning her neck, hoping, praying Rick was all right, when someone set a hand on her shoulder.

With a scream, she whirled around, already swinging her purse out as a weapon.

"Man, you are the fiercest little thing I've ever

seen,'' Rick said, ducking clear of the purse's swing.

"You have a gun."

"Yes." He tucked it in the back of his jeans. "Why the hell were you coming in? I told you to wait outside. I have to be able to trust you."

"Trust." She let out a laugh that sounded far more like a sob, and put her fingers to her mouth. "I am not sure we share the meaning of that word."

His mouth tightened, but he said nothing else.

"I do not like guns."

"I do. Ah, hell." He stepped closer and stared at her with accusation. "You're shaking." He was shaking, too; she could feel his hands, the ones that were back on her arms now, holding her steady.

But not against him, where she suddenly wanted to be.

"S-someone went through my things."

He made a low, rough sound, and his hands tightened on her, but he still didn't draw her close. She wanted to be held against that strong chest. She wanted to be stroked and told everything was going to be okay. "Rick," she whispered, lifting a hand to his heart, clutching his shirt because, crazy as it seemed, he felt like her only anchor.

With another groan, he finally drew her close,

An Important Message
from the Editors

Dear Reader,

Because you've chosen to read one of our fine romance novels, we'd like to say "thank you!" And, as a **special** way to thank you, we've selected <u>two more</u> of the books you love so well **plus** an exciting Mystery Gift to send you— absolutely <u>FREE</u>!

Please enjoy them with our compliments...

Pam Powers

Lift here

Peel off seal and place inside...

How to validate your Editor's "Thank You" FREE GIFT

1. Peel off gift seal from front cover. Place it in space provided at right. This automatically entitles you to receive 2 FREE BOOKS and a fabulous mystery gift.

2. Send back this card and you'll get 2 brand-new *Romance* novels. These books have a cover price of $5.99 or more each in the U.S. and $6.99 or more each in Canada, but they are yours to keep absolutely free.

3. There's no catch. You're under no obligation to buy anything. We charge nothing—ZERO—for your first shipment. And you don't have to make any minimum number of purchases— not even one!

4. The fact is, thousands of readers enjoy receiving their books by mail from The Reader Service. They enjoy the convenience of home delivery...they like getting the best new novels at discount prices BEFORE they're available in stores... and they love their Heart to Heart subscriber newsletter featuring author news, horoscopes, recipes, book reviews and much more!

5. We hope that after receiving your free books you'll want to remain a subscriber. But the choice is yours— to continue or cancel, any time at all! So why not take us up on our invitation, with no risk of any kind! You'll be glad you did!

GET A *Free* MYSTERY GIFT...

SURPRISE MYSTERY GIFT COULD BE YOURS **FREE** AS A SPECIAL "THANK YOU" FROM THE EDITORS

The Reader Service — Here's How It Works:

Accepting your 2 free books and gift places you under no obligation to buy anything. You may keep the books and gift and return the shipping statement marked "cancel." If you do not cancel, about a month later we'll send you 3 additional books and bill you just $4.74 each in the U.S., or $5.24 each in Canada, plus 25¢ shipping & handling per book and applicable taxes if any.* That's the complete price and — compared to cover prices starting from $5.99 each in the U.S. and $6.99 each in Canada — it's quite a bargain! You may cancel at any time, but if you choose to continue, every month we'll send you 3 more books, which you may either purchase at the discount price or return to us and cancel your subscription.

*Terms and prices subject to change without notice. Sales tax applicable in N.Y. Canadian residents will be charged applicable provincial taxes and GST.

If offer card is missing write to: The Reader Service, 3010 Walden Ave., P.O. Box 1867, Buffalo, NY 14240-1867

BUSINESS REPLY MAIL

FIRST-CLASS MAIL   PERMIT NO. 717-003   BUFFALO, NY

POSTAGE WILL BE PAID BY ADDRESSEE

THE READER SERVICE
3010 WALDEN AVE
PO BOX 1341
BUFFALO NY 14240-8571

NO POSTAGE
NECESSARY
IF MAILED
IN THE
UNITED STATES

and she pressed her face to his throat, closing her eyes. His arms came around her, slowly, as if he were resisting for all he was worth. "They're gone," he said.

"They?"

"It took more than one person to make this mess." He nudged aside a fallen pot, the plant and its dirt scattered across the entrance beneath their feet.

Nina nodded as if she understood perfectly, but she didn't. He was right. She was still shaking, and she couldn't stop, couldn't stop the fierce drumming of her head or heart.

Bending, she reached for a broken frame. The picture was of her and Terry, when they'd been very young, sitting in the surf and sun. Baba was in the background, beaming with pride at their sand castle.

"I still remember this," she whispered. "I can still remember being that happy and free."

"We need to talk."

"Yes." She looked around at the devastation and drew a deep breath. "But I think I am going to be a bit busy for a while." Cradling the picture to her chest, she walked through the rooms, carefully picking her way through what looked like a national disaster zone.

"Damn it, Nina, I need the truth."

She turned and faced him, and was surprised to see his cool facade fall away, revealing his fear and concern.

For her.

Oh, yes, she wanted to trust him, with all her heart she wanted that, but old habits died hard. She needed to get to Baba, needed to talk to her, needed to see if any news had come from her sister.

If Baba still hadn't heard from Terry, then maybe, just maybe, Nina could put her trust in this man who wanted to care for her but held himself back.

CHAPTER EIGHT

RICK FELT an urgency he didn't wholly understand but wouldn't ignore. A great part of that had to do with the last time he'd allowed a beautiful, innocent woman to distract him from his job.

She'd died.

He hoped he'd started to forgive himself for that, but he knew one thing. It wouldn't happen again. He wouldn't let any sort of lust or attraction blind him from danger, because he would simply not feel lust or attraction.

Not for Nina.

It was nearly evening before the police were finished. Rick put Nina into her car and told her to wait. He didn't go far, only to the rear of the car. Leaning against it, he pulled out his cell phone.

Mitch answered on the first ring. "Tell me you found her, Singleton. That's all I want to hear from you."

"Not yet," Rick told him, hearing the fear behind the temper. "But the sister's in trouble. Someone's been watching her. Her place has been ransacked.''

''Was she hurt?''

''No, just shaken.'' So was he. His legs were still a bit weak, and if he thought about what might have happened to Nina if she'd gone home sooner, or if she'd managed to lose him in the streets of Rio as she'd so desperately tried to do, they got even weaker. ''The key to finding Terry is through Nina. I'm sure of it.''

''Okay. I'll come down—''

''No.'' Rick didn't like the panic that went through him at that. He wanted Nina to himself, a bad sign, a very bad sign. ''No need, not yet. I'm going to stay with her until I get a solid lead. Did you know Terry went to school in the States for a while?''

''No, but her English is impeccable.''

''I saw a picture of her and a friend in a yearbook. We should look up that friend.''

''Get me her name,'' Mitch said. ''I'll find her.''

''Will do.'' Rick clicked off and looked through the window at Nina, who was sitting rigidly, staring ahead.

At her destroyed condo.

With a sigh, Rick locked his motorcycle in her garage and got into her car. Dark was impending now, and he drove, dividing his time between watching the road and the horribly withdrawn expression on Nina's face as she stared blindly out the window. She was so still she was scaring him.

"Nina."

Nothing, no flinch, no darkening of the eyes, absolutely nothing. She was in shock, and he cursed his decision to play big, bad hero. He should have called a friend for her, a co-worker, anyone at all, anyone but him, and she'd have been fine.

But one look into her sweet, vulnerable face and he had taken over with a driving need to see her safe.

But he wasn't attracted to her.

Yeah, right.

"I'm taking you to my place," he said, turning out of the exclusive area of Ipanema and heading toward a far more modest part of town where he rented an inexpensive flat.

AKA hole in the wall.

"My place," he said again, but even that didn't get a reaction, and he began to worry she was in need of medical attention. He should take her to a doctor, he thought, and wondered where the hell one found a reputable doctor in Rio. He'd half decided to go hunt down one of his informants to ask

exactly that when she slowly turned her head toward him.

"I do not need you to take care of me."

"Could have fooled me. What the hell were you thinking, walking into your place after it had been ransacked?"

"Back to that again, are we?"

"What if you'd walked in on them?"

"Then I would have been able to identify them for the police."

He snorted, but inside he was quaking at the thought of her facing the guys who'd torn her place apart. "What are they looking for, Nina?"

She lifted a delicate shoulder, and he wanted to shake her.

"Want to know what I think?" he asked.

She shook her head.

"I think someone else is looking for Terry, too."

She flinched, the reaction he'd been waiting for, but what he felt was a deeply rooted fear. "You're going to have to tell me all of it," he said. "If for nothing else but to save your own pretty little hide."

That got her attention as well, and she shot him a look of daggers.

"Yeah," he said. "Wake up call. You're in danger. That's my gut instinct, and believe me, my gut is always right.''

She crossed her arms over her chest, the protective gesture tugging at him when he didn't want to be tugged at.

His cool distance was failing him. ''Nina.''

''Why do you care?''

Why did he care? Well, *there* was a can of worms.

''All that matters to you, all that has ever mattered, is finding my sister. So why do you care what happens to me?''

Because you get to me when no one else has in a very long time. ''Because I'm human, all right?''

''Humph.''

''How about, I won't walk away from you simply because you're being stubborn and stupid—''

''Stupid? *Stupid?*'' She sputtered at that, then glared out the windshield. ''You have some nerve. You are either totally blind or…or…''

''Or what?''

She looked at him then. ''Or something has happened before. With your work. You feel guilty.''

That pretty much blindsided him, and he took his eyes off the road to stare at her.

She looked right back, steadily. ''I am right, of course.''

He turned back to the road.

"Rick?"

"I'm driving."

"Was it while you were a bounty hunter?" she pressed.

He cranked up her radio until the windows were almost shaking. She reached out and turned it off. "Was it?"

"This is about *you*, not me."

"Was it before you came to Rio?" she asked, her voice softer now.

When he glanced at her again, he could see her eyes matched her voice. Both were full of compassion, empathy, and such sweet innocence—God, just like Mary Jo's—he found himself unable to speak.

She cared about him. Despite his best efforts to be distant, she cared a lot, and that was his fault, too. He didn't deserve her to look at him like that. Didn't deserve any of it.

"Rick," she whispered, laying her hand on his arm. "Tell me. I want to understand."

Her touch was like a drug, easy to swallow and majorly addictive, so much so that he actually found himself leaning toward her.

"You lost someone," she guessed.

"Yeah."

"Before here."

"She died in the States."

"You…loved her."

"Yeah." He inhaled deeply and kept driving. "I was a federal marshal before. And a SEAL before that. I was good at what I did. Until I fell for a witness and let my emotions blind me."

"She betrayed you?"

"No. I betrayed her. I slacked off on the job, thinking she was safe if she was with me. She wasn't. And now she's dead."

"Oh, Rick."

"Forget it. I shouldn't have told you."

"I am so very sorry."

"Yeah. Me, too." He said nothing else, and neither did she, until he pulled down his street. He'd taken a series of wrong turns on purpose, hoping they hadn't been tailed.

"You will not let me down," she whispered when he turned off the car. "I believe in you."

"You shouldn't."

"But I do."

He could hardly breathe. Looking at her was the most painful thing he'd done since burying Mary Jo, but she was waiting for him, open and warm and accepting. "Don't," was all he could say.

She merely let out a small smile and entwined her fingers with his.

He'd have to be a real ass to pull away, but that was what he wanted to do.

As if she knew it, she leaned close and kissed him on the cheek, her mouth soft and sweet.

"What was that for?" His voice was as harsh as he could muster with a lump the size of a regulation football in his throat. "For handcuffing us together, or for yelling at you, or for—"

"For caring." She got out of the car.

She was out in the open and he was staring after her like a love-struck teen. Swearing at his own stupidity, he scrambled out and followed her.

His apartment was on the third floor, and since the elevator rarely worked, they started up the stairs. No one ambushed them, no one followed, and for now, she was safe.

Unlocking the door, he went in first by habit, checking to make sure the place was clear.

He led her into the living room, kicking at an old sweatshirt he'd tossed on the floor. It landed under the sofa, which was also where he toed a forgotten newspaper and an old paper plate.

"It is nice," she said, and he had to laugh.

"Yeah, if you like old and used and dirty." It was dark now, so he flipped on some lights.

"It is old, yes." She looked around, assessing. "And used. But warm. It is a home."

"Face it, even your maid wouldn't live here."

"I do not have a maid. I like to clean myself."

Why was he arguing with her? He could see the exhaustion in the fine lines around her eyes. "Look, it's early, but I think you should go to sleep."

She sat on the couch and nodded, stifling a yawn.

"Not there," he said, trying not to notice how very appealing she looked sitting all cozy in his house. "You can have my bed."

Her gaze jerked up to meet his. "Rick—"

"I'll take the couch," he clarified, nearly swallowing his tongue at her unmistakable look of disappointment.

Big trouble, Singleton.

"I do not wish to disrupt your life."

"Why not? I sure as hell disrupted yours." He pulled her up, and when she stumbled, caught her against him.

She merely sighed and put her head on his chest.

The gesture, one of trust and even more, made him physically hurt. Damn it, damn it. "Nina. Don't."

"I wish you would stop with the cool and

tough.'' She lifted her face, nuzzling it against his throat. "I understand, but I wish..."

Each word she spoke had her lips tickling his skin, and the ball of attraction knotted in his gut burst into flame. "This is who I am," he said, his teeth knocking together with the effort not to grab her and hold on. "Cool and tough."

"You do not have to hide yourself, not from me."

"Is that what you think I'm doing?"

"Yes, but I can be strong, too, Rick."

Yeah, he was getting that—she was strong as hell, and it was damned arousing. He pulled back, took her hand and led her to the bedroom.

"I have it figured out," she told his back. "You are keeping your distance so you can protect me."

"The bathroom is right through there if you need it."

"I do not need protection from you."

Which left it open...what *did* she need from him? He was afraid he knew. "Call out if you need anything."

"You know what I need. You need it, too."

Looking down into her stubborn features, he let out his breath. "Don't complicate things. We're stuck with each other, at least for the night. Let the rest go."

"But—"

"If you want to talk, Nina, if you're not too tired, we will. You'll tell me everything. About Terry, and where she is. About why you've got trouble tailing you. We'll discuss it all. And while we're at it, what was the name of that friend of Terry's? The one in the yearbook?"

"I...don't remember."

"If you'd only tell me, I could find Terry and be done with all this. The end."

Her voice went cool, her eyes hot. "Good night."

"Yeah, that's what I thought." He watched her turn toward the bed, but because he couldn't handle actually seeing her climb into it, he left.

And wandered the apartment. He couldn't have shut his eyes if he tried. Not without remembering the terror in Nina's face when he'd shown up at her place on her heels, witnessing the destruction.

She was in danger, but why? And why now?

And from whom?

Sinking to the couch, he tilted his head up and stared at the ceiling, trying to put the pieces of the puzzle together, but he was missing too much.

All he knew for certain was that he couldn't let anything happen to her, not on his watch.

That she was on his watch at all really got to

him, but then again, so did her huge, expressive eyes, and the way she fit against him as if she'd been made for the spot.

Aw, hell. This was bad. Very bad.

Pushing to his feet, he paced the room, trying to put facts together. One, he'd gone looking for Terry and had found Nina. Two, someone besides him was looking for…what?

Terry?

If he and Mitch knew Terry wasn't dead, which they did, then it was a good possibility someone else knew as well.

But who? And who besides the authorities had any stake in bringing Terry back?

All was silent in the back end of his apartment, too silent. He went down the hall, just to check on her, he told himself. It had nothing to do with needing to see her, or needing to assure himself she was okay.

Still dressed, the light still on, Nina lay on his bed, curled into a tight little ball on her side. Her hands were tucked in close to her body, her mouth curved into a little frown.

He slipped off her shoes. She didn't budge.

He pulled the covers up for her, unable to resist stroking his fingers over her arm.

In her sleep, she jerked.

"Shhh," he whispered, dancing his fingers over

her cheek. He'd been so long without human touch, and though she didn't touch him back, it felt…good. "You're safe," he murmured, the heart he'd feared dead cracking. Defrosting. "You're safe."

At his voice, she turned toward him, still deeply asleep. Her frown slowly dissipated, and all he could do was stare at her.

He'd made her feel better, with just his voice and his touch.

How could that be?

He didn't want to mean anything to anyone, and certainly not her, a woman who deserved far better than the likes of him.

He didn't want her to mean anything to him, either, but she did. Somehow she did.

How had this happened in such a short time? How had it come down to him not just wanting to finish this job and find Terry for Mitch, but also making sure this woman, this amazing, resilient, beautiful, intelligent woman, was safe?

Sleeping peacefully now, Nina burrowed further in his covers. Rick sank to the edge of the bed and watched her.

A long time passed like that; Nina lost in dreamland, and he lost in the watching.

Just looking at her hurt, and he wished… Hell. He didn't even know.

CHAPTER NINE

NINA WOKE UP rumpled, exhausted and disoriented. With her eyes still closed, she stretched, but instead of luxurious, expensive silk, she felt... rough jersey cotton?

Eyes jerking open, she took in the small but masculine room, and it all came rushing back to her.

Rick.

Her apartment.

Rick.

He'd let her sleep in his bed, the entire night if the clock that read nine o'clock was any indication, and he hadn't taken advantage of her.

Darn it, what was wrong with him?

He'd withdrawn from her, no doubt about it. She'd allowed herself to hope and dream...but there was nothing for it, not now. He'd decided to be cool and distant, and as he was the most stubborn person she'd ever met, she doubted anything could change his mind.

Certainly not his past, which ripped at her. He'd suffered, and she knew that the pain and guilt were still raw for him.

It was selfish to wish things could be different, and she was so rarely selfish, but she felt it now.

Lord, her life had gone to pot. After agonizing over that for a moment, she decided to stick to her earlier plan. She'd go see Baba. She knew there was no news, but she felt the urge to see her old nanny. If only for comfort.

If, as she suspected, there was really nothing new, then she had little choice. She would trust Rick enough to help her help Terry, and hope that along with her trust, he might give her his.

With that decision made, she sat up and shoved her hair out of her face. It was time for action.

Climbing out of the big, cozy bed that smelled just like Rick, she grabbed the small bag she'd taken from her condo and headed for the shower. There were many things she would have to do today, the least of which would be figuring out exactly how to get to see Baba without Rick following her, but first a shower. In her day-old clothes and makeup, which had long ago smudged off, she felt exposed. She wasn't ready for exposed, not with Rick.

The water was hot and steamy, just as she liked

it, and she forced herself to hurry so there'd be hot water for Rick if he wanted a shower.

She wondered how he'd slept.

She knew how he *looked* when he slept. As magnificent as he looked doing everything else. All those years of chasing after bad guys, running and hiding and whatever else it was he did, had honed his lean muscular frame into a mouthwatering art form. Just thinking about it made her entire body throb. Everywhere she washed, then everywhere she dried off with his towel felt like an open, erotic nerve, and she knew for the first time in her life she had it bad.

She wanted him.

Now she understood Terry a bit better, the hunger that had always driven her sister to chase after one man or another.

And she wasn't sure she liked it.

When she had some makeup on, and a full ensemble that would be acceptable to go from seeing Baba to the office, Nina looked at herself in the mirror.

Normally she saw a cool-eyed, restrained woman, the same woman she let people see. But that woman was gone, replaced by a bright-eyed, frightened, *real* woman.

Somehow, she'd come to be...well, herself. And

Rick had seen her this way. She'd let him in past the obedient little sister-daughter-businesswoman. He'd seen her, really seen her, as no one else ever had.

She would deal with that.

Later.

First up, she had to escape long enough to do what she had to do.

She found him in the small kitchen, wearing faded, threadbare jeans and nothing else, standing at the stove scrambling eggs.

The sight of him cooking, chest bare, belly flat, hair sticking straight up, scrambled her brain as surely as those eggs in the pan.

Craning his neck, he peered at her from sleepy eyes that became instantly wide-awake and heated.

"Good morning," she said, a little breathless. His back was sleek and smooth and tough with sinew. His front was sleek, too, and rippled with strength.

She could look at him all day long and never get used to how good he looked.

This had never happened before.

Her one serious boyfriend had been in college. She'd lost her virginity to him, and then he'd moved on. She'd declined to share herself again, and had no other experience of intimacy to draw on. "Um…thank you for your bed."

His gaze traveled up her body slowly. "Did you sleep well?"

"Yes. Did you?"

"No."

"I am sorry. Was the couch too small? Too uncomfortable?"

"Yes, but that wasn't the problem."

"Problem?"

"Yeah." He set down the spatula. "Truth?"

"Uh…okay, yes."

"I couldn't stop dreaming about you sprawled out in my bed."

She nearly staggered backward at the intensity of his gaze. "In this dream…were we together?"

One brow arched to the middle of his forehead.

"Oh," she said quickly. "We were…." She was breathless. "Was I…naked?"

His green, green eyes darkened. "Most definitely naked."

She licked her suddenly dry lips. "Was I… good?"

"You were good. You were hot."

She felt hot now.

His voice was low, thick. "Last night was the

first time I've ever had a sleep-over with a woman without actually even sleeping with her.''

"Last night was the first night I ever had a sleep-over with a man, other than the night before. Which was also with you.'' She hadn't meant to say that. He made her tongue loose, he made *her* loose.

He looked uneasy. "You mean…without sleeping?''

"Period.''

They stared at each other for a long, long moment, then the toast popped up, making Nina jump.

"Hungry?'' he asked, as if he hadn't just rocked her world. "I've got eggs and toast.''

What she was hungry for had nothing to do with food, and she was fairly certain he felt the same. Not that he was going to act on that hunger, which was good.

Nerves were dancing in her stomach. "I need to get to the office.''

"Okay.'' He scooped the eggs onto two plates and, nudging her into a chair, set one in front of her. "I'll take you.''

"That is not necessary.''

"I'll take you,'' he repeated, handing her a fork. "Then I'll go pick up my bike.''

"I am going to be busy all day.''

"So am I." He shoveled in some eggs from his plate and didn't look at her.

Appetite gone, she set down her fork. "Doing...?"

"Checking out the library. Do you still have that yearbook with you?"

"Yes."

"I want the name of that friend."

"But why the library?"

"I'm going to look at any microfiche I can find of the boating accident."

He wasn't giving up. That should cheer her, make her feel as if she could be open with him, but instead, for some reason, it terrified her.

"Eat," he said, gesturing to her untouched plate.

She forced a smile. "Funny, but for a man who claims not to want anyone in his life or his heart, you sure take care of people well."

He went still for a moment, then shrugged. "I was hungry myself, that's all."

"It had nothing to do with anything else?"

A frown crossed his face. "Such as?"

"Such as maybe you care about me."

He looked at her for a long moment. "I care about you in the way I don't want anything to happen to you," he said carefully.

"But you do not trust me."

Now his smile was back. "No more than you trust me, sweetheart."

IT WASN'T QUITE as easy to ditch Rick Singleton as she'd imagined. He took her to her office as promised, but when she walked toward the building, slowly, hoping he'd vanish so she could get back into her car and go see Baba, he was still there. Leaning against the car, feet crossed.

Watching.

When he saw her looking at him, he lifted a hand and waved.

But didn't budge.

With a sigh, she went inside the building, then peeked out a window, watching as Rick finally caught a cab. She knew he was off to get his bike, then to the library. And given their archaic library system, compared with the one in States, she was satisfied he'd be gone a good long while.

She stuffed the financial file she'd brought for John Henry into his mail slot. Dodging back into the heat without checking in, she got into her car and started along the highway, becoming more and more unsettled as she drove.

No big deal, she told herself. She was just visiting Baba. No one would think it strange.

No one would think to try to find Terry through Baba.

But because that was one of Nina's biggest fears, that somehow she would lead someone to Terry through actions she considered innocent, she drove faster.

When she arrived, she parked on the street and walked up the curved, crumbling walkway to the teeny house her father had bought Baba when she'd retired. It was an old but beautiful place, overlooking the sea.

It had been Baba's only request, along with frequent visits from Terry and Nina, which they'd done until Terry's arrest. Since then Nina had stayed away as well, afraid to put a connection between the woman and Terry's disappearance.

As she climbed the stairs, she glanced at the hillside and the extensive gardens the older woman had so lovingly planted over the years. Normally the place was alive with color and growth, but the flowers were dry now, starting to wilt. Very odd, as Baba's garden was a source of pride and joy. Hurrying her steps, Nina wondered if Baba had fallen ill, and if so, why she hadn't said so two nights ago.

At the top of the stairs, she stopped short, heart in her throat.

The door was ajar.

Just as Nina's own had been the day before. A coincidence, she tried to tell herself. But as she knocked, the door swung open, revealing more terror.

No destruction, as there'd been at Nina's condo, but worse.

On the tile foyer lay the huddled, far too still form of Baba.

IT TOOK RICK an hour to get the librarian to help him. She was as short as she was round and ancient, and she spoke very little English.

Another hour was spent cooling his heels while she went painstakingly through the archives to find the requested microfiche. Just when he was about to blow his lid, his patience long gone, she reappeared.

"We close for lunch in twenty minutes," she said in Portuguese.

"I'm going to need at least an hour—"

With a sweet, uncomprehending smile, she walked away.

"Wait!" He tried to translate into Portuguese, but she kept walking. Swearing colorfully in both Portuguese and English, he took several dirty looks from the people milling around. Rick gave them

the look right back and got to work. Apparently he
didn't have time to mess around.

Ten minutes whipped by while he digested all
the information he could. Everything about the
sailing accident seemed suspicious to him. First,
there'd been warnings of an approaching storm.
Second, Terry was not a boat person. By all accounts, she'd rather lie on the beach and tan her
body than get on a sailboat, much less work one.

Alone, no less.

None of it made any sense, and as he finished
reading all the articles and accounts, he switched
to the photos given.

And hit the jackpot.

It was a picture of the investigation. They'd
pulled the wrecked sailboat in. It lay on its side on
the sand, and several authority figures had been
photographed milling around taking notes and
measurements.

Behind them, and behind the police line, was a
small crowd, all unidentified, all watching.

Front row and center was a woman who looked
haggard and full of fear. She had corkscrew auburn
curls, and was the woman in the yearbook picture
with Terry, the best friend from school. The
woman most likely to sail around the world for the
rest of her life.

A master sailor, in other words.

Not someone who would let her friend die in a sailing accident.

Damn, Rick wished he'd gone through Nina's bag and taken that yearbook, but she hadn't wanted to give it to him and he'd let it go, not willing to resort to stealing it.

He hated when his conscience got in the way of his work, and it wouldn't happen again.

Why had there been no mention of Terry having a friend with her that day?

"We are closing for lunch."

His friend the librarian again. "Yeah."

"Now, *senhor.*"

"I just need a few more—"

"Now."

Since she was still smiling at him so sweetly, he smiled back, his most charming smile. "I just need— Hey!" He stood up when she ripped out the microfiche, grabbed the box with the others in it and walked away from him. "I wasn't finished!"

She simply sent him another sweet smile over her shoulder.

Fine. He was finished. At least here. He had to hook back up with Nina and get that yearbook, whether she liked it or not. He'd find Terry through the friend. Case over.

No more Monteverde sisters.

And if something deep inside protested, if he wondered if he could really walk away from Nina, he ignored it.

SHE WASN'T at work as she'd promised. Rick stood in front of the huge reception desk of All That Glitters, watching the woman consult the logbook from that morning.

She shook her head. "No, she never arrived."

Rick was overcome with dread. He knew damn well she'd arrived, he'd dropped her off himself. "She never came in?"

"No, *senhor.*"

He'd watched her walk into the damn building himself, which meant one of two things. Either she'd somehow gotten by the receptionist...or she'd fooled him.

She'd fooled him.

Damn her. Didn't she know anything could happen to her without his protection? And where the hell had she gone? What had been so riveting, so dire, so important that she'd had to trick him into thinking she was going to work, and then sneak out?

Something to do with Terry.

She'd held back on him, he'd known that, but

he'd looked into her deep, melting eyes and fallen for the warmth and affection he'd seen swimming there.

What an idiot.

And so was she, because like it or not, she'd attracted some attention. Whether it was the person who had supposedly framed her sister or some new threat, he had no idea, but it scared him that she would put herself in danger.

Or maybe there was no danger at all.

Maybe *she* was the bad guy.

No. He couldn't be that far off the mark, not with Nina.

But she's fooled you so far, pal, hasn't she?

He wanted to think there could be any number of reasons why she'd go to such lengths to make him believe she was going to work, then not go at all.

But none of them pointed to anything innocent.

How had a little slip of a woman gotten the better of an ex-Navy SEAL and federal marshal for God's sake? He was definitely losing his touch.

And his cool.

It was happening just as it had before, with Mary Jo. He was letting his emotions in on this roller-coaster ride. A big mistake.

It wouldn't happen again.

Back on his motorcycle, he took the crowded streets as fast as he dared, making his way to Nina's condo.

The place was closed up tighter than a drum.

No Nina.

He knocked, then pounded on the door, but it didn't change anything.

Nina was gone.

Frantic, he turned back to his bike, wondering where the hell she'd gone, where the hell he'd go looking for her, when he heard her car.

She pulled up, turned off the engine and leaned her head on the steering wheel.

"Where have you been?" he demanded, stalking over to where she still sat, unmoving.

When she lifted her head, her face was paler than a ghost, her pupils round as saucers. Her mouth opened, but nothing came out.

Blood coated the front of her blouse.

CHAPTER TEN

BABA WAS DEAD. Not just dead, but murdered, in cold blood.

Nina was too numb for hysterics. Too numb for tears. Too numb for much of anything, which made it a miracle she'd managed to drive herself home.

She'd done so on auto-pilot, hardly even registering her hands directing her car into her complex, then parking in front of her condo.

The horror of Baba's murder kept flashing through her mind, threatening her shock-induced state of calm.

For the first time in her life she didn't inhale deeply of the ocean breeze or take a good long look out at the gorgeous Atlantic.

But as she caught a glimpse of her front door, and the police tape still blocking the entrance, everything came rushing back, and it proved too much, abruptly shattering the blessed numbness.

''No,'' she said, shaking her head, then lowering

her forehead to the steering wheel. "This is not happening."

But it was. Terry was missing, either in danger or worse. Baba, her beloved Baba, was gone forever.

And she was so afraid, so tired.

So alone.

Without warning, the scalding tears she'd been holding back came in a flood, but before she could even let out a shuddering sob, her door ripped open.

She might have screamed, if she'd had the time, but she was hauled out of her car and yanked into a set of strong, warm arms.

Rick's arms. She and Rick were sheltered between her garage and the open car door, where no one could see them from the street. Safe. She was safe.

Baba was not.

"Nina." His voice was hoarse, racked with fear. "My God, Nina. You've got blood—" Gently he eased her back so he could look down at her, which made him turn pale and swear.

She felt his hands skimming over her entire body, but she couldn't move, her every limb like lead.

Baba was dead.

Shot execution-style in cold blood and left to die.

Why? Why would anyone want to hurt her? She'd been nothing but a sweet, kind, very old woman who deserved to live out her remaining days doing nothing but tending to her flowers.

That she hadn't was somehow related to Terry, and therefore Nina.

Her fault.

It muddled her mind, as did the images of Baba lying dead on her tile floor.

It would haunt her to her dying day.

"Where?" Rick was demanding, hands still streaking over her. "How bad? My God, what happened to you? Nina, where is it all coming from?"

She wanted to tell him—would have, except her body felt as if it had been wrapped in ice.

Rick sank to the ground and brought her with him, cradling her in his lap while he continued to search for the injuries that weren't hers. "Nina. Nina, talk to me."

She couldn't do anything but hold on tight, so tight he had to pry her hands off the front of his shirt to examine her. She shook her head, trying to tell him it wasn't necessary, she was okay.

He grabbed her hands, pressed them to his chest. "Be still. Let me help you."

Let him help her. Yes. Yes, that's what she should have done from the very beginning, she could see that now. He was tough. Dangerous, too, but only to her heart.

She could trust him, and she would, because she needed him desperately now. "Rick—"

"Shhh," he said shakily, as though he hadn't just told her to talk to him. "So much blood, my God." His fingers shook as he undid the buttons on her blouse. He spread it open enough for him to look at her, his eyes dark and intense and so full of terror she hardly recognized him.

"Not mine," she managed to gasp.

He stared down at her torso, at her white lace bra also dotted with blood, at her breasts, which strained at the material, at her ribs, her tummy quivering with so many emotions she could hardly function. "Not my blood." Somehow she managed to cover his hands with her own. "I am not hurt."

He stared down at her for one more second before hauling her back against him. Burying his face in her hair, he held on tight. "Thank God," he murmured, squeezing so hard she could hardly breathe. "Thank God."

The embrace defrosted her, and painful as it was, she began to feel, really feel. Sobs racked her entire frame, along with the ever present shudders, which she couldn't control, either.

Still holding her, Rick surged to his feet. She wasn't sure if he *wanted* to be holding her, or if she was gripping him so tightly he had no choice. Reaching into her car, he grabbed the keys.

He let them in her front door, kicked it closed and made his way down her hall past the worst of the mess to her bedroom, which had also been searched and ransacked.

"Close your eyes," he commanded, and still holding her, sat on the bed, back against the headboard.

She closed her eyes, but all that did was give her mind a blank screen on which to paint with blood.

Baba's blood.

With a little cry, she tried to burrow deeper into Rick's body, and he let her. "What happened?" he demanded.

"Nothing happened to me."

"But *something* happened. At work?"

The way he was watching her made her wary. Somehow he knew she hadn't gone to work. "No." More grisly images flashed across her vision and she shuddered.

He let out a low, ragged sound. "Nina, damn it—"

"I went to see Baba, my old nanny. She looked after Terry and me when we were little, she was like our mother—" A sob escaped her before she could control it, and she slapped a hand to her mouth.

Rick said nothing, just waited with a stillness that told her he was good and furious at her for tricking him.

"The blood is hers," she whispered. "When I went to see her, she had...been executed. Murdered. I found her lying in her own blood, Rick, and I tried to help her, tried to scoop her up—" She swallowed hard at the memory of that cold, lifeless body in her arms. "The police said it had been at least twenty-four hours ago, which would have been right after I called her from here, right before I went to Arraial do Cabo."

His arms loosened their hold on her. His intense gaze met hers, demanding and questing. "More."

"I think she was murdered for what she knew. About Terry."

"And what she knows...do you also know it?"

"I'm not sure." She shivered again, and wished he would pull her back against him, but his distance and cool voice made her wonder if he'd ever forgive her for not telling him everything before.

Nina hated regrets, and tried not to let them creep in now. She'd done what she'd had to do, and the fact that she only now felt she could trust him wasn't something she could change. "Rick, Terry didn't die in September."

"No."

"I—I don't know where she is now. I don't even know—" her voice cracked, not moving him at all "—if she's still alive."

Oh, his eyes were cold now, weren't they, and her heart was quickly getting there as well.

"Rick—"

"*More,* Nina. I want to hear all of it."

Behind the cool distance was a man capable of compassion and affection, she knew it. She'd seen him only moments before when he'd thought she'd been hurt. Despite his tough words, his fear had only just now begun to fade from his eyes. It told her what she'd already guessed just that morning but hadn't been ready to face.

He was the one.

She could, for the first time, invest her heart. In any case, she had no choice, because it had invested itself without her permission.

"From the beginning, Nina."

She closed her eyes and tried to concentrate. "The beginning. Terry ran the business side of All That Glitters, and I handled the creative side. It worked for us, and we were happy. But one day, out of the blue, police starting snooping around Terry, watching her apartment and the office. Within minutes of arriving one morning, she was arrested for embezzlement and smuggling gems."

Rick digested all this, most of which he already knew, without a word.

"She was innocent, Rick. Obviously framed."

"How do you know this for sure?"

"I know my sister." But *he* didn't, and she could tell he wouldn't be easy to convince. "The way she lived her life did not mean she was dishonest or a thief."

"What about proving her innocence in court?"

"Our father…well, I have told you the evidence was insurmountable. He refused to believe in her. All she had was me. She was not a criminal," she said firmly. "She was *not*."

"Okay."

She searched his gaze, but couldn't decide if he believed her. "The evidence stacked against her was tremendous. Staggering even, though she was let out on bail. She…ran."

Rick slanted her another long glance. "Didn't trust in the law?"

"She could not. Whoever framed her was good, the law would have failed her."

"So she vanished, without even a word to you?"

"She assured me she would get messages to me somehow, and she did."

He nodded, looking very unhappy with her. "Through this Baba."

"Yes." Nina shivered again and wrapped her arms around herself. "A few months later Terry let me know she was going to fake her death, which she did."

"In the boating accident that never was."

"Yes."

"Who helped her? Family?"

"No. Our mother died in childbirth with me. Our father is an invalid. There is just me, but she did not ask."

"Her friend helped her, then. The friend from school."

"Jolene Daniels? Probably." *Definitely.* "When I went to get the so-called body in Texas, a man met me. We never spoke. I came back with a forged death certificate and had a funeral. I buried sandbags, but to the cops, to our family and business associates, to everyone, she was dead.''

''Yet she contacted you regularly.''

''Until about a month ago, when all correspondence stopped. I have been going crazy, wondering what is happening to her, but I have no way to get a hold of her. I thought Baba—'' She closed her eyes, opening them again when he put his hands on her arms.

He'd hunkered before her, his face close to hers. ''Obviously something has happened, Nina. You're being followed, Baba is dead, and you've heard nothing from Terry. You're in over your head here, you know that.''

''I know now.''

''It never occurred to you that whoever framed her was still out there?''

''Of course!'' she cried. ''But the police here are not like your American police. They cannot always be trusted, not when they are poorly paid and can be bought so cheaply. I paid private investigators all year. They looked into everyone around us, but nothing. No clues, nothing.''

''So Terry had to stay away.''

''You believe me,'' she breathed, joy and relief battling for first place.

He just looked at her.

"You do! I can see that you do."

"You should have told me all this from the beginning."

"I did not know if I could trust you! But I do now," she said softly, knowing she was looking at him with her heart in her eyes, but she couldn't help it.

He seemed decidedly less than thrilled with her proclamation. "Don't trust anyone, *especially* me."

"But I have told you everything now. And you have told me everything."

He said nothing.

"Rick? We can trust each other now, right?"

He didn't look at her. "I'll help you find her."

"Thank—"

"For Mitch," he clarified.

"But..." Just that fast, her relief faded. "Not for me."

"Damn it." In one explosive movement, he surged to his feet and paced the room. When his gaze landed on her, his eyes softened for one brief flash before shuttering again. "You're still shaking. Stop it."

"I am trying."

Rick swore again, in fluent Portuguese this time, before stepping into her adjoining bathroom and turning on the shower. Storming back into her bedroom, he stood before the bed, hands on his hips. "Get in the hot shower before you go further into shock and I have to get you to a hospital."

"I do not—"

"You've got blood all over you, Nina. You're getting in if I have to haul you in there myself."

The thought of standing up, then removing her clothes and getting into the shower seemed like such a huge effort. She was still contemplating it when he scooped her up in his arms and deposited her in the quickly steaming bathroom.

When she just stood there, he let out a growl of frustration, then quickly and efficiently started stripping her. First her shoes, then her stockings, which he had to slip his hands up her skirt to get to. As he worked them down his jaw tightened. "Are you going to help?"

Automatically her hands went to the buttons on her blouse, but they already were open. It took her a moment to remember Rick had spread her blouse apart to check for injuries. It slipped off her shoulders, and at the same time he tugged at her skirt and slip.

In the mirror she caught a glimpse of herself wearing nothing but a bra and panties, and it shocked her. Her cheeks were flushed, her nipples pebbled, straining against the lace of her bra.

Rick was kneeling at her feet, staring up at her with the hottest look of pure hunger she'd ever seen. "I hope to God you can take it from here," he muttered, coming to his feet and backing away, hands shoved into his pockets.

She shivered, and because it wasn't with shock, she turned her back, holding her breath, wondering if he'd leave, or if he'd press close and do as she more than half wanted and touch her.

The bathroom door shut, giving her the answer to that question.

Alone, she finished undressing and stepped into the shower, standing beneath the spray, her body pulsing.

The water turned tepid, then icy before she finally cooled down enough to get out.

WITH HIS BODY fully aroused, and his thoughts in the gutter as far as one Nina Monteverde was concerned, Rick paced the floor of the condo, listening to the shower.

She'd told him everything she knew, or so she claimed.

Oddly enough, he believed her. That wasn't what bothered him.

He hadn't told *her* everything.

She'd been in shock, he told himself, she needed time.

A bunch of garbage.

He'd held back for purely selfish reasons. Self-defense. If he kept something to himself, she'd be good and furious, along with deeply hurt. She'd hate him.

And with that hatred, nothing could ever come of this ridiculous attraction between them.

We can trust each other, she'd said.

God, the open, warm hope in her eyes when she'd said that. When she learned the truth, that only one of them had come clean with the other, and it hadn't been him, she'd look at him with her heart all over her face.

Her *hurt* heart.

He should have told her, before her shower, where she was probably right this very second soaping up, running her hands over the body he couldn't get out of his head.

When his cell phone rang, he leaped for it, grateful for the diversion from his own torturous thoughts.

It was Mitch. "Just got your message."

"Where have you been?" Rick stared at the bathroom door. "I called you last night."

"Yeah, well, things are a bit wild here. I resigned."

"From the FBI?"

"Yeah. I've been swamped going through debriefing and finishing up files." His voice lowered. "What have you got?"

"Plenty."

The shower stopped. Rick pictured Nina, dripping wet and sleek and perfect, stepping out of the stall. Pictured her opening the bathroom door and giving that just-for-him smile that seemed to be able to tip his heart on its side. Pictured her opening her arms and her own heart.

To him.

Only he didn't deserve that or her, and he had no one to blame but his own fears. Wasn't that a laugh?

Big, bad, tough Rick Singleton afraid of a woman.

"Rick?"

So much for not getting personally involved in a case. So much for not letting anyone touch him or his emotions.

He was an idiot.

"Yeah, I'm here," he said into the phone. "The friend I told you about? Her name is Jolene Daniels. She might still be in Texas. I want to fly out of here and go talk to her."

"You think she'll lead you to Terry?"

"I know she will."

"Jolene Daniels…Dallas…nothing." Rick could hear Mitch flipping pages, probably of a phone book. "San Antonio…nope. Here! Perfect. Got her," he said. "She's in Houston."

Rick scribbled her address down.

"I want to go with you," Mitch said.

"Fine. I'll leave tonight. Tomorrow morning at the latest." He kept his eye on the door. If Nina did come out, naked by some miracle, he would simply close his eyes.

He would not, under any circumstances, get caught by temptation. He would not sleep with her.

He would not multiply his sins against her.

Nina did indeed open the door. Surrounded by steam, covered in a white fluffy towel, she looked like the sweetest, sexiest, most amazing woman he'd ever seen. Her chestnut hair, usually restricted, was wet and loose and flowing to her shoulders. Her eyes were dark and warm, her olive skin gleaming and shiny.

He'd never wanted anyone more.

But he'd as good as lied to her.

And she'd hate him for it.

He needed to remember that. "I'll see you soon then," he said to Mitch and hung up.

"What's that about?" Nina asked.

"I'm flying to meet Jolene Daniels."

"I am going, too."

"No—"

"Jolene will not talk to you without me." She stepped toward him, her body scented like heaven.

"Nina—"

"I have access to the company jet." She stopped a breath away, close enough that he could see the pain and grief in her eyes, but more, too. God, so much more. Close enough that he had to close his own eyes because her open trust killed him.

He'd never worried about what someone thought of him before, but he worried now, because suddenly it mattered.

She mattered. "I don't think—"

"I am going," she repeated.

Yeah, she was going. Because who the hell was he kidding? He couldn't let her stay here by herself. She looked so utterly alone, so devastated…and much as he wanted to deny it, at the moment, he was all she had.

She needed him.

The least he could do for her was be there.

And if truth was to be told, he thought maybe he needed her, too, just for a little bit longer.

Then he'd find a way to be alone again.

Somehow.

"Nina—"

"I will make the arrangements." She turned away before he could grab her, before he could haul her close, spill his fears and kiss them both into oblivion.

And in that moment, he couldn't remember why he'd done this to them, why he'd held back. Why he hadn't trusted her.

AN HOUR LATER, they were on Rick's motorcycle, heading out of town toward the airport. That they were traveling with only two backpacks was a testament to his considerable negotiating skills, since Nina had packed a huge trunk for their trip. Where she'd expected him to put it was beyond him, but he'd convinced—and cajoled and bullied—her into letting him pack for her. Now she'd plastered herself to the back of his body, holding on tight as he drove through the crowded streets.

He could feel her thighs surrounding him, her breasts boring into his back. But it was her hands, clenched low on his belly, that really drew him.

She trusted him.

She was trusting him when she had no business doing so.

He was such a jerk.

They couldn't fly out until first thing in the morning. The jet wouldn't be ready before then, according to one of Nina's employees, Meg Turner, who was making the arrangements for them.

But they couldn't stay in Nina's condo, either. The place only served as a devastating reminder to Nina of her losses, and compounded her guilt for not doing something sooner.

Rick told her not to waste time feeling guilty, but he understood that emotion all too well.

But where to go before they flew to meet first Mitch, then Jolene Daniels?

His place was out, because God only knew who was watching it now.

They'd settled on holing up in a hotel room by the airport until morning. No one would know where they were, and he could keep Nina safe.

But could he keep his heart safe?

CHAPTER ELEVEN

NINA DIDN'T KNOW where she expected Rick to take her, but it wasn't the luxurious hotel they pulled up to.

"What?" he asked, reading her surprised expression. "You'd rather a motel?"

Motels were an institution in Rio, never to be confused with hotels. Rented by the hour, for short stays only, a motel was a solution to the lack of privacy caused by overcrowded living conditions. Their clientele included adults who still lived with their parents, kids who wanted to get away from their parents, parents who wanted to get away from their kids, or couples who needed to be alone to have wild, hot sex.

When Rick just continued to look at her, she blushed. "This is good."

The room had two beds, which was a good thing, Nina told herself. She was lost in grief and fear, and she desperately needed her rest before tomorrow's trip.

But as she crawled into the cold, stiff sheets a short while later and closed her eyes, she realized rest was as far away and as out of touch as her sister was.

Flipping over, she smashed her face into the pillow, but the images that had been loitering in the corner of her mind for hours now came flying back.

Blood and gore and death.

With a small cry, she squeezed her eyes tighter and tossed onto her back. Opening her eyes, she expected to stare at the ceiling, and instead looked into Rick's green, green eyes. A lock of his dark hair had fallen over his forehead as he leaned over her.

"You okay?"

Unable to speak, she nodded, then changed her mind and shook her head.

"Is that yes or no?"

No, she indicated with another shake of her head.

A sound escaped him as he sank to the bed at her hip. "Go to sleep."

Another shake of her head, and yet another sound of frustration came from deep in his throat. His jaw was tight and chiseled, his body tense. He was at least 180 pounds of pure hunger and muscle, and she knew with his dark and dangerous good looks he could have any woman he wanted.

If only he'd admit he wanted her.

"You're not even trying," he said, skimming his fingertip over her eyelids. "Stop looking at me. Close 'em." He stroked her face in a dreamy gesture until she relaxed, but when he pulled back, she opened her eyes again.

"*Nina.*"

"My whole world is upside down."

"I know."

"Rick...help me."

"How?"

"Tell me everything will be okay." She lifted a hand to his cheek. "Make me feel it. You can do that for me."

"I am not going to have sex with you."

"Then make love to me."

"God." He pushed to his feet, shoved his fingers into his hair and turned a slow circle. "You have no idea how I want to. Or how wrong that would be."

Hope and joy combined as a heady rush, and tossing back the covers, she came to her feet as well, standing before him in a T-shirt and bare feet. "Show me."

"No!" He backed away from her, this big, bad,

tough guy who could be terrified by the thought of true intimacy. "I will not."

"Now who is not using contractions?" she teased, taking another step.

"Stop right there," he said, holding up his hand. "I mean it. You're hurting and vulnerable and there's no way in hell I'm going to take advantage of that."

"I am asking you to."

"Yes, but you're an innocent. You don't know what you're asking."

"I am not an innocent." At his dubious glance she growled, "I am not! I have…done this."

"Done what exactly?"

"Done…you know."

"Had sex? How can I believe you when you can't even say it?"

"I have had sex!"

"Yeah? How many times?"

She sighed and looked away. "Once."

"Once! That's an innocent." He looked at her. "Did you come?"

Her face went hot, and she tripped over the words. "What does that matter?"

He closed his eyes and tipped his head heavenward. "You didn't."

"That is not the point!"

"What is?"

She slid her hands over his chest. Beneath his shirt, his muscles leaped and quivered, thrilling her. "It is simple," she whispered. "Make me forget everything else. That Baba is dead and that my sister..." Her voice quavered. "That my sister could be."

With a grimace, his hands came up to her waist, squeezing gently. "Nina—"

"I have nothing at the moment but you, Rick."

"You're shaken," he said a bit desperately. "Anyone would be. You want comfort and I'm the closest guy, but I'm not that big an ass to—"

She pressed her body to his, her face to the crook in his neck where she fit as if she belonged there.

She *did* belong there. "Please," she whispered, sliding her arms around his neck.

He groaned, then wrapped his arms around her tight. "This isn't right, you don't know—"

"I know all I need to about you. You are alone, too, and though you think you are totally unlovable and do not deserve anyone in your life, you are wrong. So wrong." Gliding her lips along his throat, she thrilled to his shiver and the sound of his low, gruff groan. "You are a good man, Rick.

The best. I know you do not want me to care about you, but it is far too late.''

Going with instinct, because it certainly wasn't experience, she bit his jaw, forcing that sexy sound from him again. "I care," she whispered. "So much. Please care back, Rick. Please?"

"Nina," he breathed, burying his face in her hair. "I'm not a good bet. You shouldn't trust me, I—"

"You can tell me all your bad habits later," she promised. "Right now I just need this…this connection." And she did. Having him against her, she could feel his strength, his heat…his erection.

She was a grown-up; she knew this wouldn't last, but she wanted whatever part of him he could give her. Letting go of him, she reached down, grabbed the hem of her T-shirt and pulled it over her head, leaving her standing there in nothing but a pair of panties.

His gaze devoured her, and he swallowed hard. "You're not playing fair."

"I know." As she watched him watch her, his face twisted with barely managed restraint, and her insides went soft and pliant, melting and aching in ways that went far beyond the physical need. But physical need was what she'd created in him, and for now, it would be enough. "Do not make me beg."

His eyes were deep, so very deep, and slowly he shook his head, reaching for her hand, pulling her back against him. "I'm the one who should be begging." One hand cupped the back of her head for his hot, hungry kiss, the other splayed low on her back. His fingers stroked up and down, up and back down again, dipping into her panties to cup and hold her against him.

Still kissing her, he walked her backward to the bed until the mattress bumped the backs of her knees.

For a brief moment, nerves flickered within Nina. Not that she'd changed her mind, but that it was going to happen. Here. Now.

Finally.

"Lie down, Nina."

She did, arching up beneath his hot, hungry gaze, feeling a heady urgency she couldn't quite contain. He pulled his shirt over his head, tossed it to the floor. Then came the pop of the button on his jeans, and the metal on metal glide of his zipper as he shoved off the rest of his clothes.

He put a knee on the bed, still staring down at her as he crawled up her body. "Second thoughts?'' he murmured, dipping down to glide an openmouthed kiss along her neck.

''No.'' She gasped as skin met skin. His thigh brushed against her leg, settled between hers, opening her to him in a way that left her feeling vulnerable. Vulnerable and strong.

So strong.

Her pulse shot up and she sank her hands into his hair. ''No second thoughts,'' she repeated, dragging his mouth back to hers. She ran her hands down his back, marveling at his smooth, hot skin, at the hard, strong muscles. His body lay heavily over hers and she moved restlessly against him, wanting more, wanting to feel him lose control, wanting to feel his body inside hers, wanting so much she could hardly contain it.

His mouth left hers. She moaned at the loss, then felt the tickle of his hair over her collarbone, the heat of his lips as they closed over her breast.

Sensation after sensation pelted her. His hot tongue rasping her nipple. The thrust of his knee high between her legs. His work-roughened hand dancing over her belly, then lower, slipping into the heat of her. The glide of his fingers as he stroked the tender, swollen flesh between her thighs. The growl in his throat as he found her moist enough to sink into.

She nearly jerked right off the bed.

"You're going to come this time," he promised.

She sucked in a breath. "Yes." Her body arched, her legs opened wider, letting him have his way. She flexed her hands over his back, and he trembled beneath her touch.

With wonder she blinked up at him. "You are shaking."

"I want you, Nina."

He wanted her. He had passion and need and hunger for her, and the knowledge lit a fire unbridled until now, a fire that wouldn't go out. Not this night.

His fingers were working magic on her, something simple really, just a steady, soft stroking, but it made her wild. "Please, please," she breathed against his neck. "I need—"

He knew what she needed, and gave it to her before she had to put it to words, pressing just a little harder, a little deeper, and within seconds, she was writhing beneath him, crying his name, pulsing around his fingers.

"Another," he commanded. Lying between her thighs, holding her open to him, he gave her exactly that, made her come again.

And then again with his mouth.

Catching her breath, she stared at him in dazed

wonder as he climbed up her body, towering over her.

She was still shaking.

Never in her life had she felt so...so desired, so needed, and she opened her arms, drawing him down to her.

Holding her gaze, he reached down, guiding himself to her opening, easing himself inside her a fraction, just enough to rip a groan from his throat and a welcome cry from hers.

He pushed himself deeper, and then deeper still. The fit was tight, the friction ecstasy as he slowly pulled out, only to thrust in again.

Her mouth opened, she could hardly breathe. "Rick—" She arched her hips up to meet his. "This is good for me."

He let out a laughing groan. "It's good for me, too."

"I mean this is good for me. With you."

He went still, looked into her face. "I know."

Their rhythm was as old as time. Perfect. And in an unexpectedly tender gesture, he cupped her face, whispering her name in a voice of hushed awe. She whispered his back, just as awed. Impossibly, he grew even harder, and quickened his thrusts.

Wrapping her arms around him, she held on,

meeting him stroke for stroke until it all exploded again, together this time, bigger and brighter, all the more intense with him buried so deep within her, and just as lost in the impossible pleasure.

Eventually she came back to earth and found herself plastered against Rick's side. Her body still occasionally shuddered from the incredible lovemaking, her heart soft and melting with so much emotion she could hardly stand it.

She didn't dare put it into words.

His body was slick and hard and warm. His hand had curled around her almost possessively, making her feel...safe. Closing her eyes, she pretended they could stay this way forever.

Forever.

She liked that, and along with feeling languid and incredibly sated, she realized she was sleepy... so very...sleepy.

"Nina."

"Hmm." Maybe he was going to tell her now. Maybe he'd say the three little words she'd never heard from anyone, but would be so welcome from him.

She needed to wake up for this, but she couldn't, she felt so...relaxed. The events of the past few days had just caught up with her, that's all. Her eyes wouldn't stay open, and actually, she wasn't sure if that was really exhaustion, or from having her first orgasm.

Orgasms.

Either way, she really wanted to hear him. Couldn't wait to hear him, because with this out of the way, they could do anything.

Together they would face this mess and survive. *Together.*

Oh yes, she liked the sound of that, and for the first time in her life, her heart opened up. Her soul stirred.

And she yawned widely, her brain drifting off without permission.

"Nina, it's about Terry."

She opened her eyes again, though it was a huge effort. She found his gaze on her, no longer dark with passion, but with an intensity she found unnerving. "Terry?" she asked, her voice thick, her tongue unruly.

"I told you I came here to find her."

What did this have to do with what they'd just shared? "Yes." She sighed, smiling, yawning again, her brain fuzzy. "You came to find Terry."

"For Mitch," Rick added. "Nina?"

"Yes…because he loves my sister. Very sweet."

Something flickered in his eyes. Regret? Guilt?

Whatever it was, it vanished in a flash, replaced by a disturbing emptiness. "Yes," he whispered, dragging her close. "I think he loves her."

Her eyes were heavy, so heavy, and she tried to stay awake, but it was an uphill battle.

"Nina?"

Sleep had claimed her.

DAWN CHASED the night away, and after having watched Nina sleep for hours, Rick sank his fingers into her thick hair, stroking until she stirred. "I have to tell you the rest," he whispered.

Eyes still closed, she stretched like a cat and smiled. "There's more? Why do you not just show me?" Reaching out, she ran her finger down his chest, down, down—

He grabbed them. "Not...that." His heart was in his throat, but he couldn't hold the words back any longer. "Wake up, okay? Last night I should have... Aw, hell. I need to tell you everything I didn't before. Nina, Mitch has Terry's baby. *Their* baby."

Her eyes flew open. "Mitch has...*what?*"

"Someone left a baby at the apartment building where he's staying in San Antonio." He was nervous, he'd never been so nervous. "A paternity test proved it was Mitch's. Doing the math, he figured the mother had to be Terry. There—there was no one else during that time for him.''

Nina sat up and tugged the sheet over her body. Her hair was wild, her eyes right on his, wide with confusion. ''Terry had a...baby?''

''Yes.'' He reached for her arm, but she pulled away.

''I do not understand, Rick.''

''From what you've told me,'' he said more quickly now, realizing he wasn't going about this right, ''your sister's on the run, possibly from real gem smugglers. Fearing for the baby's life, she left it with Mitch.''

''She left a baby—*her* baby—with Mitch?''

''Yes. It—''

''You keep saying *it*.'' She got out of bed, keeping the sheet around her so that Rick could no longer see the body that had taken him to heaven and back during the night. ''A baby is not an it.''

''She. Hope. Nina—''

''You knew this, these past few days? That Terry had a baby? You knew this and kept it from me, even after last night?''

''Yes. I...'' He frowned when Nina walked into the bathroom, and he leaped up, but not fast enough.

She shut the door in his face.

"Hope," he heard her whisper softly, sounding devastated. *Destroyed.*

"That's the name Mitch gave her." He stood there with his palms on the door, bare-ass naked. "Nina." God, how had this happened? "Let me in."

"You should have told me, Rick."

Yes, he should have. Playing with the handle that didn't budge, he said, "Open up."

"I do not think so. No." Her voice cracked, killing him.

"Nina—"

"Why did she not bring Hope to me? I would have died to protect that baby!"

Rick's blood ran cold at the thought. "Which is exactly why she didn't. She was protecting both of you. Nina, open up."

"Why? So you can handcuff me again to get your way? Wheedle more information out of me for your case? No, Rick Singleton, you are through using me."

He'd really done it this time. "I didn't do this to hurt you—"

"I know." Her voice was so soft he had to put his ear to the wood. "It is because you did not trust me. Maybe you thought I had my own sister arrested? Framed? Maybe you thought that she was on the run from *me?*"

"No. No, I never thought that."

"Then why?"

"Why didn't I trust you? *You* didn't trust *me* until last night."

"Because you kidnapped me!"

This was stupid. He wanted to see her face, wanted to haul her close and bury his face in her hair and be forgiven. He wanted to make her understand it wasn't her, it was *him* and his own irrational fears that had held him back from her.

God, wasn't this a joke. Somehow, while busy protecting his life, his emotions and his heart, all three had ganged up to play some sort of cosmic joke on him.

They had turned on him and opened up to Nina.

Whipping around, he shoved all ten fingers through his hair and stared out at the calm ocean. What had happened? When he'd first come to Rio, his life had been as calm and placid as the sea. Yes, there'd been danger and excitement and thrill, but that had been his work, and work no longer touched him.

But now his life was no longer peaceful, not even close. Nina had walked into it and turned it upside down with one shy, beautiful smile.

At a soft gasp, he jerked around and found her standing in the now open doorway, fully dressed.

Her eyes were on his body, wide and dilated, reminding him he was still stark naked.

She turned away. Grabbed her bag. Headed for the door.

"Wait," he said, leaping after her.

"I do not think they allow naked people to fly."

At least she was still coming with him. Unless— "You're going to wait for me."

She studied the ceiling.

The floor.

Anywhere and everywhere but him.

"Nina." He grabbed her arms, shook her slightly until she looked at him. "You're angry. I get that. I deserve all your fury and more, I know, but damn it, wait for me."

A slight shrug was his only answer, and he had to trust that even as angry as she was, she wasn't going to be stupid enough to try to go after Terry without him.

With one last look of warning—which she completely ignored—he grabbed his clothes and headed into the bathroom.

"You didn't trust me until last night," he called out. "I'm just slower than you, okay? Nina?"

"I did not hold out news about a *baby*."

He shoved his clothes on as fast as he could. "No, you only nearly got yourself killed. *Twice.*"

"At least I trusted you as soon as I knew I could. You only trust me out of guilt."

He came out of the bathroom to see her standing by the door, smoke still coming out her ears. "Look," he said. "Before we go, we should finish this—"

She opened the door of the hotel room and walked out.

"Or not," he muttered into the thin air before following her. But he stopped her outside. "We're talking on the flight, Nina. Because we both know your pride is what's hurt here. Terry didn't come to you. That's what this is about."

She yawned, making it clear what she thought of that.

"On the plane," he repeated firmly. "We talk."

THERE WAS A JET waiting for them at the designated airstrip. The pilot, a man in his early forties, took a sip from a can of vanilla cream soda before tipping his hat to nod at Nina.

She nodded curtly back and got onboard without looking at Rick.

Rick followed the stiffest spine and squarest shoulders he'd ever seen.

She was still not speaking to him.

The pilot didn't speak either as he prepared for takeoff.

Before Nina could sit, Rick took her arm and forced her to face him. The look of utter misery on her face almost did him in. "I don't know what's ahead," he said, and because he couldn't help himself, he stroked her cheek. "But we'll get through this."

Her eyes misted and his gut twisted.

Trust me, he wanted to tell her.

But the words wouldn't come.

CHAPTER TWELVE

NINA WAS NOT a stranger to flying—she'd been in this company jet many times over the years, zipping all over the world to collect gems and unusual designs. Africa, Europe, Asia, the States...she'd been everywhere.

Normally she loved flying, and thrived on the freedom she had to travel anywhere she chose, often spending the time in the air with her drawing pad, doodling ideas for new designs.

But since Terry's disappearance, her life had completely changed, and due to her extra burdens with the business, she'd stayed in Rio.

There was no joy in this first trip in too long, nothing but fear and angst.

And, she had to admit, if only to herself, there was hurt pride, too. Rick had been right on that score.

Even knowing it was impossible, she couldn't help but wish Terry had brought the baby to her.

A baby, she thought, both her stomach hurting and her heart twisting. Her niece.

Oh, how she wished Terry had been able to trust her.

The plane rumbled through the air, low enough to avoid any commercial jets on the route. It allowed an incredible view. As the beaches of Rio gave way to the mountainous terrain of northwestern Brazil, heading toward Texas, Nina tried to relax, but with Rick watching her every move, it was impossible.

They'd made love, and just as the romances all claimed, the earth had moved.

Only he didn't trust her, anymore than Terry had.

When she felt his touch, just his fingers on the back of her hand, she closed her eyes, but all that did was allow the rest of her senses to kick into overdrive. She imagined she could taste his kiss, smell his delicious, undeniably male scent, see his smile.

"Still mad?" he asked in the same low tone he'd used to coax shockingly erotic things out of her only the night before.

She didn't answer, as she honestly didn't know what she was.

"Yeah," he said for her. "You're still mad."

More minutes passed, long minutes where, due to the lower altitude, Nina sightlessly watched the scenery morph again, from mountains to the Amazon rain forest. There was nothing beneath them now that remotely resembled civilization as they knew it, and she shivered. Right beneath them were more kinds of wild animals than anywhere else in the entire world.

After a while, the Amazon River came into view, wide and calm and deceptively serene, surrounded by nothing but the emerald broadleaf evergreens that formed the top layer of the forest as far as the eye could see. Not so much as a single bridge marred the second longest river on the planet.

"Talk to me, Nina."

She kept her eyes on the view. "And tell you what, exactly?"

"Anything."

"I do not believe you want to hear it."

At the first conversation in nearly an hour, the pilot glanced at them over his shoulder and Rick shot him a fulminating look.

The pilot reached for his can of soda and hastily turned away, making a show of downing the rest of his drink, keeping his face forward.

"It is not his fault," Nina whispered.

"I'm well aware of who's to blame here, thanks." Rick shifted closer. "God, Nina, forget him. Tell me you hate me. That Terry hurt you. Tell me that you're hungry, tired...*anything* at all, just talk to me."

"Okay. I hate you, Terry hurt me, and I am definitely hungry and tired."

The pilot made a sound that might have been another strangled laugh.

Or a snicker.

"I'm sorry about not telling you sooner." Rick glared at the back of the pilot's head. "But from the very beginning I told you I was out for myself, remember? I told you I was on a job."

"I suppose you deserve a medal for that honesty."

"I kept you safe."

"Only because you needed me."

That took him aback. "You...don't really think that."

She just lifted a shoulder.

"Nina." He sounded devastated. "No."

"I understand. I held back, too, remember?" And she'd never regretted anything more. Maybe if she'd been more open, he would have been as well, and they wouldn't be at this impasse she didn't know how to get around. "It is just that..."

"What?" He touched her hand again. "Please, tell me."

She stared at him. "You have never said please before."

He blinked, then grimaced. "Proof positive I'm an ass."

Nina shook her head, unable to resist the pull of his green eyes, deep, dark and conflicted. "I do not hate you."

"But you said—"

"I just...I thought we had something. For the first time in my life, I really thought it."

At the pity that crept into his expression, she felt the heat flush her cheeks, but she had to finish. "I let myself hope and dream that everything might be different...with you."

"Oh, Nina."

Closing her eyes, she swiped angrily at a tear that escaped. "And I feel really stupid for that."

"No, you're not the stupid one—"

Again, that choked noise came from the pilot, and this time Rick craned his neck around. "Hey, what the hell's your problem? This is a private conversation—" Breaking off with a startled oath, Rick leaped forward, just as the pilot slumped in his seat.

The plane took a nosedive.

With a scream, Nina lurched forward against the restrictions of her seat belt, nearly smashing her face into the pilot's seat in front of her. Just as quickly, the plane pitched upright, overcorrecting, throwing her back into her seat so hard her teeth rattled.

Dizzy, nauseated, she looked up to see Rick leaning over the far too still pilot, his hands on the controls. "What are you doing?" she cried.

"Flying." His mouth was grim, his eyes straight ahead. He stood in an awkward position, reaching around the seemingly unconscious pilot for the controls, every muscle in his body tense and delineated beneath his clothes. "Do you know CPR?"

"What?" Fear nearly strangled her when the plane dipped again. Then yet again.

Nina struggled to sit upright, to blink past the dizziness to focus. She saw Rick reach down and unhook the pilot's seat belt, stepping over the body when it hit the floor. Sitting in the now empty pilot's seat, he glanced quickly over his shoulder. "You okay?"

"You are…flying."

"Yeah."

Again the plane jerked, violently, so that Nina thought her seat belt would tear her in two. "Rick!"

"Come here."

"Wh-what?"

"Come here!"

Easier said than done since the plane continued to dip and rise like a roller coaster, up and down, and also side to side as Rick struggled to regain control. She could hardly get her fingers around her seat belt to release it.

"Hurry, damn it."

"Hurry," she repeated, crawling on the floor to the front, grabbing Rick's leg to steady herself. Poking her head up, she looked out the window to find that they'd lost altitude. Her stomach leaped into her throat. "Do you know what to do?"

The plane dipped again, knocking her into Rick's lap. At the feel of his tense, powerful thighs beneath her, she jerked back, nearly landing on top of the prone pilot on the floor. "Have you done this before?" she cried.

He was busy fighting with the controls.

"Rick!"

"I've seen it done a few times."

He'd seen it done. Something was rolling around at her feet and she stared at it. "There is a soda can with foam coming out of it."

"Empty?"

"Yes."

He looked down at the pilot, then let out a string of obscenities. "Does it smell like almonds? Never mind, don't touch it! How is he?"

She reached for the pilot. "He's not moving. What do I do?"

"Is he dead?"

She stared down at the man in growing horror. "How do I tell?"

"Check for a pulse."

"Check for a pulse. Checking for a pulse. *Meu Deus,* there is no pulse!" She didn't know his name, but he'd worked at All That Glitters for several years, and he'd always been courteous. Did he have a wife? Children? This could not be happening. "Rick!"

Rick closed his eyes briefly, then leveled his intense gaze on her. "Okay, listen carefully. We're losing altitude."

She could only stare at him.

"I'm not sure how to stop it."

All the air left her lungs.

"Get back into a seat belt, Nina. Now."

She peered out the window at the lush, green Amazon jungle beneath, the jungle that was currently rushing up to meet them. Vertigo swamped her, but she shook it off and crawled back to her seat.

"Are you in?" he yelled back.

"Almost. Rick, are we—"

The plane dropped and tipped to the side, throwing her against the wall. Her face hit, hard enough that she saw stars.

"Nina, seat belt! Now!"

He was craning his neck to peer out the windows, searching to the front and the sides of him with a deadly calm as he worked the controls with a sort of aim-and-miss method that made her very grateful she wasn't prone to motion sickness. "Seat belt," she repeated, afraid she knew the answer to her question, but she asked anyway. "Are we going to make it?"

"Hang on." The plane shuddered and let out a horrendous noise. He had to shout to be heard. "We're going down."

"Do you know how to land?"

There was a thin line of sweat running down his temple, his mouth was tight. "Don't ask me anything you don't really want to know."

He didn't know how to land.

By some miracle they'd stopped dropping out of the sky, but they flew low, too low, the belly of the plane brushing against the wild, lush growth that made up the jungle, stretching out as far as the eye could see, without a break in sight.

"There is nowhere to put this thing down!" she cried. "We will never make it!"

"Never say never."

The airplane pitched brutally, throwing her weight against the restraint of the seat belt, cutting into her chest, her ribs, until she was sure she would simply snap in half.

"This is it," he yelled back. "Tuck your body, cover your head with your arms. Don't look up until we stop."

She started to tuck, then stopped. "What about you?" He'd never found the time to hook his seat belt, she thought with a surge of panic. "Rick! How will you protect yourself?"

"Nina, damn it, tuck!"

She tucked.

The plane dipped again, and she bit her lip so hard she tasted blood.

They were going to die.

She'd never really imagined dying, but she was suddenly sorry she was going to do so before they'd worked through their problems.

She didn't want to die like this. She didn't want to die at all. She hadn't had kids, or gone scuba diving. She hadn't told her father she loved him.

Or Rick.

"Nina?"

She started to look up, but remembered his directions. She stayed tucked.

"Nina..." Rick sounded different now, frantic for the first time. "Nina, I'm sorry."

She closed her eyes against the onslaught of regret and anguish.

So he didn't want to die at odds with her, either. "I know."

"I should have told you."

He was only saying that because he thought they were going to die. They were hitting the tops of the trees now. The plane shuddered and made a horrendous noise. Nina was thrown left and right, then left again, her entire body pummeled from all directions, and she bit her lip again, not wanting to distract him by crying out.

The noise was atrocious. As Rick took the plane down through the thin canopy of trees, they hit hard and fast, bouncing up off the ground twice more before smashing down for the final time, sliding through the thick growth and headlong into a tree.

AFTER ALL the earsplitting noise, the silence was deafening. In that silence, Nina heard Rick's last words.

I'm sorry.

I should have told you.

Should have.

Should have.

Those last words echoed in her head over and over, until suddenly it occurred to her.

All was still. *Too* still.

Everything felt like a dream. Even her own breathing, so harsh in the quiet, seemed surreal. Lifting her head, she opened her eyes.

And at the sight of the dead pilot, on his back at her feet, eyes and mouth open, tongue hanging out, she screamed.

The sound bounced around her head and in the plane, but there was no answer. The fog blurring the edges of her vision faded, and so did the sense of being asleep.

She was horribly wide-awake, not dreaming at all.

Where was Rick?

Fumbling with her seat belt, she freed herself. She tripped over the pilot and landed on her hands and knees in the front of the plane.

Rick lay slumped forward, and didn't move when she sobbed his name. Scooting closer, she placed her hands on his back, leaning over him, looking into his face.

His eyes were closed, which was a good thing,

since blood was pouring down his temple from a long, jagged gash on the top of his head. "Rick!"

"Told you…" His lips barely moved. Nothing else did, either. "Told you…I'd seen this done."

A laugh escaped her, but it was purely hysterical. "You need medical attention. Stitches for certain."

"Got…any thread?" Somehow he managed a smile, though it was a weak one. "Come on, it can be your revenge. Stitching me up without drugs."

The thought made her feel like throwing up, but then he shifted and groaned.

"Don't move," she said quickly.

"Not…planning on it."

"My God. What are we going to do?" He was fading fast, not moving at all. His eyes were still closed, his color far too pale. Frenzied, Nina craned her neck around and surveyed the wreckage around her.

It was bad. One side of the plane had been sheared right off, leaving them exposed to the elements, which happened to be Amazon jungle in the hot, sticky midmorning.

She could see branches tangled together. Thick vines curled around trunks and dangled from limbs. The foliage was so thick that very little light reached through, and already insects had discovered them.

Who knew what other creatures were hovering just beyond?

"This is really bad," she whispered. Figuring Rick would come up with a good quip for that, one that would probably annoy her but at least banish her fear, she looked at him.

He didn't so much as budge. In fact, he hadn't moved or said another word.

"Rick?"

Nothing.

The man was a thorn in her side, a brooding, rough-and-tumble man afraid of nothing but his own emotions.

A man she'd had the bad luck of falling in love with.

But furious as she was at him for all of the above, she wanted him to open his eyes and flash her his cocky smile. She wanted him to tell her everything was going to be okay.

She wanted him to hold her tight and be the strong one, but since he didn't move and nothing was okay, nothing at all, that job looked to be hers.

"Rick." She touched his back, his neck, searching for a pulse, which she found with a grateful sob, but the fact that he was deeply unconscious, possibly dying, prevented her from throwing herself over him. Afraid to worsen his injuries, she stroked his hair and once again looked around her.

She was truly alone in this, she thought, then nearly leaped right out of her skin at the screeching bark of a howler monkey.

The air came alive with noises then, cries and hoots from hawks, vultures, and many other unknown creatures, all of which made her scrunch tighter within herself.

Seems she wasn't quite so alone after all.

RICK WOKE to a screaming headache and a sweet, soft coaxing voice.

"...all you have to do is wake up, Rick, yes?" Something silky brushed his face. "And anything you want, I promise. Just please wake up."

"That'd be...worth coming back from the dead for." He licked his dry lips and cracked open an eye. Nina leaned over him, her hair tickling his jaw. He managed to pop open the other eye. "Did you really say...anything I want?"

"Oh, Rick!" She flung her arms around his neck and squeezed, hard. Her body slammed into his and she lay over the top of him, shaking like a leaf. "I thought you were going to die—" She squeezed harder. "And I could not help you and—"

As she squeezed, serious pain shot through him, through every single inch, and Mr. Tough Guy that he was whimpered like a damned baby.

"Oh!" Nina eased back, just a little, and beamed at him, though her smile was wet and wobbly. "Sorry."

His throat was parched, his head hurt like a son of a bitch, and that was before he tried to sit. Gasping, he struggled, then finally managed to sit up with her help. "I feel as if I've been in a plane wreck."

Her smile faded. "That is not funny."

"I know." They were still in the plane; he could see that. She'd managed to get him flat on the floor, or maybe he'd landed there himself. All he remembered was her scream and the control panel rushing up to greet his forehead, all personal-like.

Near his feet lay the pilot, and the gritty details, such as murder and bad landings, came back to him. For the first time he got a good look at Nina, or as signicant as he could through a haze of pain and a good amount of sweat and blood blurring his vision, but what he saw made his heart twist. Lifting a hand that felt as if it weighed a million pounds, he touched the growing bruise on her jaw and cheek, regret and fear making his voice hoarse. "You're hurt."

"Not like you."

Not believing her, he ran his hand down her arm, tugging her back against his side so that he could search the rest of her for himself. Her limbs moved around him easily enough, but when he touched the ribs on her right side, she sucked in her breath hard. Tears came to her eyes.

"Just bruised," she whispered.

"But they hurt like hell," he guessed, pulling her closer, welcoming the pain because at least they were alive.

But the empty soda can on the floor spoke of deadly intentions. Even now he could still smell that faint scent of bitter almond, which he knew from his SEAL days was cyanide. His guess was someone had offered their pilot that drink knowing the heavy taste of the poison would be masked by the vanilla flavor of the soda. And once their pilot died in the air, everyone else would die as well.

Without Rick's lucky landing, that is. "Much as I'd like to make you repeat that promise to me—"

Nina blinked. "Promise?"

"That you'd do anything, anything I want…"

She blushed. "As always, you speak inappropriately."

"There's nothing inappropriate about what I want, believe me."

She stared at him, her eyes wide and troubled, reminding him there was still a world of differences between them, not the least of which was that she was a forever sort of woman.

And he no longer did forever.

But suddenly, looking at her, that seemed rash.

And even, somehow, a chicken way out. His life was lonely.

Incomplete.

He'd definitely hit his head too hard. "Help me up."

"I do not know if you should be moved."

"We need to get out of here."

"But you need medical attention!"

"Nina, do you see an ambulance waiting for us?"

They both looked outside to the lush, green overgrowth of a Brazilian jungle.

"Do you see a highway, or even a hint of civilization?" he pressed. "Anything?"

Her eyes clouded. "No."

"It's just you and me, sweetheart. Just you and me."

She didn't look thrilled, and he couldn't blame her.

He wasn't exactly thrilled himself.

CHAPTER THIRTEEN

By now their plane had gone down, courtesy of a nicely reliable poison.

Nina Monteverde and Rick Singleton were dead, which should have brought a rush of pleasure, but there was no relief at all from the all-consuming need for revenge.

Because Terry was still missing.

But she would be found. No matter what, she'd be found.

And finally, vengeance would be had.

NINA FOUND HERSELF sitting in the middle of the wreckage, blankly staring around her. Logically, she was in shock. She'd been in shock for days, it seemed. She couldn't quite escape the fog.

Rick looked as if he suffered from the same shock. His eyes were wide and slightly unfocused, though that could be his head injury.

What if he'd died?

Like their poor pilot. At the reminder of him, her entire body tightened in grief.

But Rick was still alive. He was still in her life.

Not that she wanted him there, but it was out of her hands. Like it or not, he was firmly encroached in her heart and soul.

She must have made a sound because he whipped toward her, his face lined with worry. "What? What's the matter?"

Only that she loved him. "I—"

He let out a short, mirthless laugh. "*What's the matter? Can you believe I asked you that?*" He came close, pulling her against him. "We have to do something."

"Yes." But she'd rather stay like this for a good long while first.

"Our equipment is out. No radio. And no way are the cell phones going to work. We filed a flight plan, but as the plane is now beneath the tree canopy, it'll take forever for anyone to find us."

They were about as isolated as they could get and still be on earth.

She watched Rick push to his feet, then wobble crazily. She thrust her shoulder beneath his arm to steady him. "What are you doing?"

He tossed her a smile but it didn't meet his eyes. "I'm thinking we need to get on the move. I don't know about you, but spending the night here isn't my idea of five star accommodation.''

''But…will they not come find us?''

''They?''

''Officials. Someone. Anyone,'' she added weakly at the sympathy in his eyes.

''Nina. We didn't come down in the best of places.'' Squeezing her shoulders, he let go to teeter his way toward the back of the plane, where he pulled out first the plane's emergency supply kit, then his backpack. He dumped the contents of his pack out, only to toss selected items back in it such as water, a snake bite kit, bug repellent and dried food. ''We'll be able to load just my backpack with what we need.'' He stopped to swipe the blood that was, still oozing into his eyes, and took a moment to rub his temple. ''If we're lucky, we'll find help within a few days.''

''Days! But…''

''Cover him.'' He tossed her a blanket and gestured toward the dead pilot. ''We'll do what we can to make sure someone can get back for his body. Good, there's pills for malaria.'' He opened the drugs and pulled out a bottle of water. ''Take two of these right now.'' He did the same. ''We'll take more, for as many days as it takes us.''

Meu Deus. Malaria. Snakes.

As many days as it takes.

"Here's a tent." He let out a grim smile, but his relief was clear. "We're styling now."

A tent.

As in camping.

Only she'd never camped a day in her life. Overwhelmed by the magnitude of it all, she just stood there.

Rick stopped filling the pack and looked up at her, his eyes dark and intense. "We should hurry."

"Why?"

He dropped his gaze and began working on the pack again, tying the small, tightly wound tent— the one that didn't look big enough for him alone, much less the two of them—to his pack. "I hope your shoes are comfortable."

She looked down at her leather flats. "Yes, but…Rick?"

He sighed. "Look, we're alive, right? Let's keep it that way."

They took care of his head injury the best they could, and did the same for her lesser injuries.

Then they climbed out of the plane. That alone took great effort as they were deeply embedded in bush. Rick had to cut branches away so they could leap down. He went first, and though he jumped, lithely hitting the ground, he sat for a long moment afterward, holding his head.

"Rick!"

"I'm okay." But he was green when he stood, reaching to help her down.

Around them, trees and plants grappled for space in the hot, damp perpetual summer climate. They set out walking, Rick looking down at the compass he'd found in the survival kit. Around them broadleaf evergreens made up the main tropical growth. There were tree ferns as well, tall with delicate crowns some as high as a six-story building.

And though it was the middle of the day, the light had to filter through the growth, which muted it to early dusk.

By dark, it would be terrifying. The whole situation terrified Nina. "You know there are lots of hungry creatures out here in the jungle, right?" She craned her neck, checking to make sure none of those creatures were following them.

"We're hungrier."

"I do not know, the capybara eats a lot."

He slowed and looked at her. "Capybara?"

"A hundred-pound rat."

"Oh, that." He swallowed hard and started moving again. "Nina?"

"Yes?"

"Stay right behind me."

"Okay. Have you seen an anaconda before? They are forty feet long—that is the height of a four-story building in case you were wondering. They swallow their prey whole. Keep your eyes out for one of those."

His back and shoulders were wide, strong, beautiful. And very tense. "Nina?"

"Yes?"

"Watch where you put your feet."

She watched her feet and followed him.

And followed.

It seemed they walked forever and a day through the tropical vegetation. The ferns, grasses and other flowering plants had all attained great height and volume, sometimes taking on strange shapes that fed her imagination. There was bamboo too, some only several inches high, some giants more than 120 feet.

Exhausted, Nina looked at her watch. They'd been walking only three hours.

Rick never slowed, and she couldn't help but feel there was more to his urgency and desperation to get them to safety than he had indicated.

Not that he was talking.

He was in front of her, whacking his way through

the heaviest growth with the biggest pocketknife she'd ever seen—which he'd taken out of his pant leg.

"How many more weapons are you hiding?"

"Plenty," came his grim reply, reminding her that this man truly lived on the edge at all times.

More hours passed. Soon it would be nightfall. Rick was breathing hard, too hard in her opinion, and his head was bleeding again, right through the strip of cloth they'd ripped off the hem of his shirt. "Rick, we have to stop."

He looked at her, his shirt damp and clinging to his body, his eyes dark and intense. Around him, lianas and woody vines, some as thick as a man's body, hung like cables. An alien world, yet he looked at home. She had a feeling he'd look at home anywhere. Only she could see the pain he struggled to hide, and the exhaustion.

"You're not okay?" he asked.

She was, she supposed, but he wasn't, not that he'd admit it. He needed to rest. "I need to lie down."

His expression assured her she hadn't fooled him, but he complied. They found a small clearing, and together set up the tent, which was the size of a postage stamp. "We cannot both fit in there," she said, knowing neither of them could rest without the dubious protection of the tent.

"It's meant for at least four people." Rick nudged her in and followed. "We'll manage."

Yes, if they were on top of each other.

When they were both inside, on their knees, facing each other, Rick shook his head. "Okay, it's a tight fit." He looked shaky, and she scooted as far back as she could before opening his pack and taking out some water and crackers.

"Lie down," she said gently. *"Please,"* she added when he would have resisted. Taking the matter out of his hands, she helped him stretch out, then fell against his side when he tugged on her.

"You lie down, too," he said, opening his arms. "Come here."

His body, hot and hurting, felt solid and familiar beneath hers. He was there for her, which was more than she could say about anyone else in her life. Overwhelmed, she wrapped herself around him, and he held her with his big, warm hands, allowing her to bask in the closeness. "Rick…"

"I know. You feel good." He pressed his face to her throat. "Good and alive. I like that in a woman."

Making a satisfied sound of agreement, she slid her hands beneath his shirt, seeking more of that warmth because she couldn't seem to get enough. Somehow, he took the emptiness from deep inside her, the emptiness threatening to swallow her up, and filled it.

"When I first realized we were going down," he said against her skin, "all I could think was, I had to keep you safe." He hugged her hard. "And I couldn't."

She closed her eyes to the reassuring masculine sound of his voice. "But you did." Her body hummed now, with something much more than fear, and she pressed even closer. "You did."

In the wake of the terror they'd survived, his holding her was a relief, but a pleasure, too.

Suddenly more pleasure than relief.

"Rick…"

He groaned, and when she might have backed away, he pulled her tighter to him. "Not yet. Don't go away yet."

He'd been hurt. He didn't trust. Maybe he never would. There could certainly never be a future between them without that trust, but she couldn't walk away.

Not yet.

"Nina." His mouth nuzzled at her ear. "Hold me."

"I will. I am." She was on his lap, straddling

him so that she could feel every hard, perfect inch of him. The slow burn in the pit of her belly took flame, and she couldn't have stopped the gentle rocking of her hips to his erection to save her life.

He gripped her tight, urging her on, coaxing her body to fit itself to his in an attempt to put out the fire.

She could feel the pumping of his blood, or maybe that was hers. There'd be no resisting, not now, maybe not ever, at least not on her part. Much as she knew pulling away to be the smart thing, her body simply wouldn't, couldn't, and driven by this overwhelming desire and hunger, she closed her eyes and let it take her.

He touched her, and everywhere he did, she smoldered for more. Her breasts, her belly. Between her thighs.

Her head spun with the unrelenting need.

Somehow his jeans opened. Somehow her skirt bunched up around her waist. Somehow her hands were in his shorts, touching him. He was fully erect, needing release, and she was equally desperate.

"Have to…" He gripped her bottom in his kneading fingers. "Have to feel you."

"Yes. Now." Shamelessly panting, shamelessly wet and ready, she rubbed herself over him.

They were both lost then. He pulled her down on him, smoothing her panties aside to let him in. "Like this, Nina, here—" With a low, rough sound, he guided her over him, while she tore at his shirt buttons so that she could open her mouth on his bare chest. When he slid into her, they both let out a long, gratifying moan, and then again when he thrust into her with rising fervor, using his fingers, his mouth, everywhere, until she was a quivering, heated mass on the very edge. Knowing her inside and out now, as no one else ever had, he easily drove her off that edge, flying with her, and they both came with a long, thready cry.

Stunned, shaken, they sank together and let sleep claim them.

NINA CAME AWAKE to Rick holding her close, his mouth to her ear. It was nice, and she snuggled in.

Then he whispered, "We're going to get out of this, Nina, I promise you," and reality came back all too quickly.

With a sigh she opened her eyes and took in the dim light that told her it was very early morning. Her entire body ached, and thanks to waking up every hour or so to check on Rick, she still felt exhausted. "A promise." Her hands were slow to leave him. "And here I thought you never made them."

"I don't." Over her head, he frowned. "That is, I don't make any I can't keep."

"I never asked you for any promises."

"You should." His hands streaked up and down her back, not a gentle, tender touch, but a solid, life-affirming one, and she gripped him back just as hard, looking right into his eyes when he cupped her face and tilted it up. "You should be asking me for all sorts of things," he said, looking unhappy with himself.

He had no idea how much that only made her care all the more. "Such as?"

"Commitment. Marriage." His mouth went grim. "Love."

"Since you say that as if it is a dirty word, you will excuse me for not asking you for a thing. Especially that." With another sigh, she shifted off him. "I guess we ought to get moving again."

He looked at her, concerned.

He wasn't going to let this go, and she had no intention of letting him know she'd so stupidly fallen for him. "Rick, we have known each other for less than a week. Did you think I expected commitment, marriage and love after such a short time?'' She lifted a shoulder. ''Just concentrate on getting us out of here.''

''Nina—''

''Come on,'' she said, reaching out a hand, not wanting him to look too closely, to see she wanted exactly those things she'd just scoffed.

He stared at her for a long moment, so long she feared he was going to push the issue, but he took her hand.

AROUND THEM the jungle was a study of motion and sound. If it was sunny or raining or cloudy or even all of the above, she had no earthly clue, since the sky couldn't be seen through the thick growth around them. Nina felt as if they'd penetrated some secret green facade as they wound their way through a maze of unbranched trunks that soared upward, their crowns indistinguishable among the high latticework of foliage. Flowers were everywhere, wafting a heavy fragrance when the wind blew.

''Watch out for that nut tree,'' she said worriedly as Rick passed it. The entire thing was filled with heavily encased pods of nuts. If one of those landed on his head, it would surely kill him.

Or her.

She had no idea how anyone could find their

way out of this place, but Rick had a compass and he said he knew what he was doing, that if they kept walking this way, they'd eventually come to the Amazon River. Once on the river, they'd be able to flag down help.

Probably.

That word, and all the others, which included poisonous snakes, hungry caimans—a relative of the alligator—and deadly insects, were jumping around in her brain.

So was exhaustion.

Every few minutes, Rick would turn around and just look at her.

"What?" she finally asked, dripping in sweat, sore and aching, and not feeling particularly charitable toward the man who wouldn't say what was in his heart. "What do you keep looking at?"

"You."

She saw things in his eyes, things she'd dreamed of, like warmth and affection, and as they had to be a mirage in this endless heat and humidity, she got mad. "Well, stop it. You are giving me ideas."

"Ideas?"

"Ideas that would make you run screaming."

"Like?"

"Oh, no," she said on a mirthless laugh. "I will not go there, just to be told—politely, mind you—

that you do not do those things. I already know that, so just…just stop looking at me.''

"Nina—"

"*Walk,* Rick. We will get nowhere standing here, miserable in each other's company.''

"I didn't know we were miserable in each other's company.''

"Pay attention then.''

His jaw tight, he turned around again.

Silent.

As they walked this time, he didn't look back.

"RICK?''

He didn't want to turn around, didn't want to see the exhaustion and temper in Nina's eyes. Didn't want to feel his heart tug good and hard as it did every time he so much as thought of her, which was only every living second. He hacked at a long, winding branch. "Yeah?''

"Why did the pilot die?''

He'd wondered how long it would take her to put the clues together. How long before she came out of shock enough to realize they were in far bigger trouble than any crash landing in the middle of the Amazon rain forest.

"You should be saving your energy.'' Stopping, he searched the immediate area around them, which was nothing but green, green and more green. A virtual wall of dense growth garlanded with hanging lianas.

Oh, and the heat. He couldn't forget the over-whelming, all-consuming, drenching heat.

But he'd paid damn good attention while crash landing, and with the help of the compass, he could get them to the river. From there, they'd pay some-one to take them to the closest village.

Theoretically anyway.

"You are keeping things close inside, as al-ways," Nina said, miffed.

Yes, it was a special talent of his. "We're get-ting closer to the river. But I think it's still several miles off. And we—"

"Yes, yes, we have to get there before nightfall because if we are lucky, we will find a village, or at the very least somebody to borrow a river boat from. You have said. Several times. But what you have not said, Rick, is a word about the plane and the way we were forced to land. What happened to our pilot?"

Tipping his head back, he studied the sky. Or what he could see of it between the high canopy of trees. "He died."

"I know that." When she caught up with him, she tugged on his sleeve. "Why?"

She honestly didn't know. She was either too innocent or just not thinking clearly. God, she was sweet. Too sweet to be caught up in this mess, whatever this mess was. Certainly far too sweet to be involved with him, but suddenly, he couldn't imagine what his world would be like without her in it.

After only a few days of knowing her.

Talk about terrifying.

"Rick?" She was cupping his face now, peering into his gaze worriedly. "What is it? You just went pale as a ghost. It is the pilot, I know it. You are hiding something new from me now?"

Yeah, he was hiding something. Big time.

He was hiding the fact he'd not only allowed his frozen heart to defrost, but let her climb right in and make herself at home, opening him to all sorts of emotions and feelings he wanted nothing to do with. "We need to keep walking."

"Damn it!"

He stared at her in shock. "What?"

"Yes, I swore! I do that occasionally, when extremely frustrated." Her fingers grabbed the front of his shirt. "Now, I realize you cannot wait to get rid of me, but—"

"What?"

She blew a stray hair out of her face. "Are you

really hard of hearing, or are you just being as irritating as possible on purpose?''

She looked furious. And magnificent. If his head didn't hurt like a mother, and if they hadn't been in danger from a million different things, the least of which was dehydration and exposure, Rick would have grabbed her and quite possibly never let go. "I most definitely *can* wait to get rid of you."

Her eyes narrowed and she opened her mouth, but he set a finger to it. "And our pilot was poisoned. That's what the foam on the soda can was. And that bitter vanilla smell. Cyanide, and we were all meant to die on that plane because of it. Now before you use another swear word, understand something. I didn't tell you because I didn't want to scare you. Silly, yes. Macho and egotistical, double yes. But I feel an accelerated possessiveness toward you that seems to force me to act stupid."

"He was poisoned," she said dully, less than underwhelmed by his admission of not wanting to get rid of her.

If that didn't beat all to hell. "Did you hear what I said?" he asked.

"Yes, someone killed that poor man. Someone tried to kill us." She looked back over her shoulder. "No wonder you did not want to stay with the plane. What if they came to check their handiwork?" Her eyes were huge when she turned back to him. "Who would want us dead?" She clamped a hand to her mouth. "The same person after Terry! It is the same person who framed her, it has to be! Do you know what this means?" Once again, she gripped his shirt tight. "That all we have to do is catch this person, and we will be able to prove Terry's innocence!"

He shook his head. "Whoa. Back the tuna truck up. We're not catching anyone. You—"

"If you say I am not experienced enough to go after this person, or able to take care of myself, I will—"

"Nina." He grabbed her arms. "I said I feel something for you, and—"

"Well, bully for you," she snapped, stepping back and crossing her arms. "Welcome to my world."

"What does that mean?"

"It means I hope to God you care for me—we have slept together twice! I care for you, too, you asinine, closemouthed, impossibly stubborn *Americano!*"

Thoroughly baffled, he narrowed his eyes.

"What does being American have to do with anything?"

She threw up her hands. "Someone is trying to kill us and suddenly, *now,* you want to open up and talk?"

"Okay, yes, someone is trying to kill us. But since I'm not going to let them—"

"See?" she cried, pointing at him. "That is exactly the chauvinistic kind of thing I would expect you to say. I do not want your guilty need to protect me, I want—"

Stepping forward, he hauled her up to her toes so they were eyes to eye. Unfortunately they were also mouth to mouth. "My wanting you safe has nothing to do with guilt," he said very quietly.

"Really?" Her eyes were smoldering. "What *does* it have to do with?"

"Damn it, that's what I'm trying to tell you!" He was confused enough to muddle everything up. When she wiggled against him, he groaned and pulled her snug to his body.

At the feel of his erection, she sucked in a breath. "Is that the danger making you excited? Or me?"

"You!" he shouted.

She sagged against him, wrapping her arms around his neck. "Oh, Rick. Do not let anyone kill you. I like you alive." She nuzzled her face against his neck and breathed him in, making his knees weak. "I like it a lot."

Sighing, he hugged her close, marveling at the fact he didn't want to let her go.

Ever.

"Nina…" Ah, what the hell. "I like you alive, too." He closed his eyes and held on, having no idea how he was going to let her go when this was over.

He opened his mouth to tell her so, his heart pounding with nerves, when suddenly Nina gasped and pulled away. "We have to hurry!"

"Yes, but—"

"Someone went to a lot of trouble to kill us. And whoever that someone is knows where we were headed, right? They must know about what we were going to do." Her fingers dug into his shoulders, her eyes filled with terror. "My God, we have led them right to her."

"Jolene Daniels."

"Yes! We have to get to her first! Then we have to find Terry and warn her, too! Before it is too late."

He looked into her angst-ridden face, the face he'd come to dream about day and night, and let out his pent-up breath.

CHAPTER FOURTEEN

"DID YOU KNOW forests cover half of Brazil?" Nina asked. Nightfall was only moments away now. Hot, sticky and thirsty, she tried to distract herself from this impossible situation.

Rick walked in front of her, clearing the way when he had to, grabbing any large heavy branches, holding them back for her to walk through unscathed.

She'd rather he turn and grab *her,* but how unrealistic. She'd committed the ultimate mistake, she'd fallen in love. And she'd done it with a single-mindedness that shouldn't have surprised her.

The problem wasn't whether Rick could feel that way in return. He had a heart, a big one. She'd seen him panic over her well-being. She'd seen him deep in the throes of passion. She'd seen him every which way. He cared, she had no doubt.

But he didn't want to.

And ultimately that was what would keep them

apart, because when she loved, she loved forever, and she wanted it to go both ways.

They'd reached the river an hour ago, and were currently making their slow, painstaking way downstream through the bush, hoping to come across a clearing in which to be safe through the night.

Rick hadn't spoken in hours.

She wished he would say something, anything. "In these forests, it rains something like two inches a day," she said. "It all eventually flows into the Amazon."

He grunted and swung the knife. His shirt clung to the muscles of his shoulders and back as he worked with a strength and determination she knew to be an innate part of him.

"Not that you would want to be right on the banks of the Amazon," she said, turning a wary eye on the water. "The piranhas come out this time of day. They are nothing but teeth and bad attitude. Oh, and then there are the giant, bloodsucking leeches that latch on to a human host at any available opportunity."

He didn't break stride.

"They love human blood."

"Nina?"

Finally! "Yes?"

"Are you going to talk all the way there?"

"Probably."

She got another grunt.

Frisky monkeys and brilliantly colored birds darted in the overhead canopy, while millions of insects droned all around, heard but not seen thanks to their effective camouflage.

Rick kept slapping at his neck, making her worry. She didn't often get stung by anything—she didn't have sweet blood, Terry used to say—but if Rick was getting stung, and if he developed a reaction, it could be bad. "You getting bit?"

"Only everywhere."

"Pull up your collar a bit."

His disbelieving laugh vented the air. "We lived through a crash landing. You probably have two cracked ribs and a damn near cracked cheekbone. I have a slice out of my head and a concussion to boot, and oh yeah, we're racing against the clock and a cold-blooded murderer, and you're worried about a mosquito bite?"

"Take more of those malaria pills."

"I did."

"Maybe we should stop so you can eat something."

"You're talking to me as if I were a cranky child."

"Well, if the shoe fits..."

"So you *are* going to talk all the way there."

Oh, that was it. Moving toward him, she jabbed a finger in his chest. "At least I am *trying* to get along! You just bully and boss your way through life or jungle, never worrying or wondering what other people think, and—"

"I don't give a damn what other people think, that's true." Snaring her finger in his hand, he tugged, and when she fell against him, he grabbed her and held on. His eyes were hot and fierce and so was his voice. "But I give a damn what you think. Did you know that? I give lots of damns, and I tried to tell you, and all you wanted to talk about was this stupid case that I'm wishing I never took on!"

Her heart had taken off, slamming against her ribs. Or maybe that was his. "Is that right?"

"Yeah." He grimaced and slid his jaw to hers. "You're killing me, Nina." His arms tightened around her. "I want you to forgive me for not telling you about the baby, for—"

"For not trusting me?"

Slowly he pulled back. "Yes."

"I told you I understood, and I meant it. After all, trust has to go both ways, right?"

"Uh...yeah."

"Yeah." She started walking again, this time leading the way.

FOR A MOMENT Rick just stared at her. Then he realized she was disappearing into the thick growth and he stumbled after her, swearing when a branch slapped him right in the face. "Nina, wait!"

Naturally, she didn't.

"Damn it, wait!" he yelled. "I want to talk to you."

"You mean you want to yell at me."

"No, I don't. And about that untrusting thing—" Another branch slapped him in the face, and yet another moment was taken to swear colorfully. "Would you *stop!*"

Amazingly, she did, but kept her back to him. Coming up behind her, he stared down at her bowed head and the exposed sweet spot on the back of her neck. "Okay, maybe I have a few issues. Being stubborn and untrusting among them."

She snorted, and he slowly shook his head. "But you have the same issues, sweetheart."

She let out a long breath. *"Did,"* she agreed. "But not so much anymore."

"Really? You completely trust me?"

"With my life," she said simply, making him

feel weak and strong and humbled and terrified all at the same time.

"I'm working on doing the same," he said very quietly.

She didn't move, which he took as a good sign. The way his blood roared in his ears was a sign, too—a sign to get on with this and get it over so he could breathe again. "Remember what you said on the plane about you wanting there to be something between us? You said that you wished that more than anything." He reached out and stroked that spot on her neck, the spot he wanted to nibble. "I want that, too."

"Wanting is easy." She was walking again, at such a fast clip, he was left dodging flailing branches.

"I more than want," he called after her.

"Uh-huh." She ducked beneath one branch, then stepped over another.

"Look, I'm trying here!" He struggled to keep up with her brutal pace while jackhammers were going off in his head. "You think it's easy running and talking and spilling my guts all at the same time?"

She slowed slightly.

Taking heart in that, he gulped in some badly

needed hot air. "I'm tired of living with regrets and hollow emotions."

Though she kept moving, and didn't look at him, he could tell she was straining to catch every word.

Love swamped him. "And as for the trust issues thing," he said, "if I didn't trust you, would I be chasing your pretty butt through this mess?"

She slowed even more, then came to a halt, and he had to smile.

She was waiting for more, and he knew he had to give it to her. For the first time he could. "And since I now so completely trust you, I'd sure as hell like to accept your trust as well."

Slowly she turned to him, her face carefully blank.

"With anything. Everything," he said.

Her gaze searched his. "You are sure about that?"

"I'm very sure."

"Well then, you should know, I really do trust you. I think I always have, I was just afraid."

"Afraid of me?" The thought made him sick. "I never meant to scare you." He thought of the handcuffs and grimaced. "I mean, I—"

She laughed. "Oh, you meant to scare me, but that is just it. I always felt safe with you, even then, odd as that is. I was just afraid of what you make me *feel*. Kiss me, Rick.''

Yeah, that would work, and he eagerly stepped close to do just that. Cupping her face, he tilted it up and first looked into her brown, melting eyes. "I want to tell you, Nina, you're it for me. Heart and soul. Now that you've taught me to live again—"

Her eyes shimmered. "I taught you that?"

"You did." He slid his thumb over her scrumptious lower lip, already anticipating their next kiss. "I love you."

She dragged her teeth over that lower lip, her eyes full and so bright he could see himself reflected back. "No one has ever said that to me before," she whispered. Letting out a little laugh, she spun around, then went rock still, her back to him.

"What?" he asked hoarsely, feeling as if he were hanging from a cliff with a rope about to give. "What is it?" Damn it, he wanted to hear those three magic words echoed back to him.

"We're here." Clapping her hands, she whirled around to face him. "Look, a *malocas,* a communal house." She pointed it out just ahead. "A farm, Rick! And they have a dock and a boat!

We're saved! We can get to a town and call Jolene. We can find Terry!''

But where was her declaration of love? Couldn't she see he was dying here? ''Nina—''

''And food.'' She rubbed her belly. ''I bet they have food!''

''Nina.''

''Hurry!''

He caught her just as she would have danced away. Hauling her close, he gripped her hips, being careful with her ribs, but he really wanted to finish here. He wanted her to look him in the eyes.

Then she did. And went utterly still. Slowly she reached up and touched his jaw. ''Rick? Why are you not happy?''

''You have to ask?'' He let out a hollow laugh. ''I've just dumped my heart at your feet, along with my pride, and you say nothing in return except 'let's go eat'?''

Her fingers slid over his jaw into his hair, carefully avoiding his injury. ''Are you saying I did not answer you?''

''That is what I'm saying.''

Her lips touched his, softly, sweetly, and when he would have deepened the kiss, she pulled back. ''Such an oversight,'' she said, eyes brilliant.

''Was it?''

Her smile came fast. "Oh, enough. I cannot tease you, I love you too much."

He stared at her. *She loved him too much.*

She loved him period!

"Rick?" Her finger rimmed his ear, and his body went immediately hard.

"Yeah." He cleared his throat. "You…love me too much."

"Well, of course."

"Damn it, say it right," he demanded.

She laughed again and hugged him tight. "I love you, Rick Singleton. I love you with everything I am and everything I will be. Now tell me again."

"I love you. Don't ever forget it."

"You could tell me often. That would help."

He smiled. "How about every day for the rest of your life?" He hadn't known that was sitting on his chest, waiting to be said. But instead of terrifying him, it felt right. So right he said it again. "Every single day. With me. Can you handle that?"

A tear spilled. Her smile dazzled. "I can handle that. I want it, too, Rick. So very much."

He kissed her mouth, and would have added his body into the mix, but the lure of the farm proved too much for both of them.

Together, their arms around each other so that

neither knew who supported whom, they tramped forward, knowing that whatever lay ahead, they would face. Together.

Forever.

RICK KNEW THEY needed to get to Jolene Daniels. Knew they had to still find Terry, and reunite her with her baby and Mitch Barnes. That had been his promise to Finders Keepers, and he always kept his promises.

But he wanted Nina safe. It was all he could think about.

It took two days.

The farm they'd found had provided shelter, but frustrating little else in the form of modern technology. They ate and slept there that night, then the next morning paid one of the men to take them down the river in his boat.

Which turned out to be little more than a raft.

Finding anything other than crocs and insects took another long day and night, and the entire time Rick's neck itched.

Someone was following them.

Impossible, he knew, but he wouldn't feel good until he had Nina on a plane headed toward the States. As a result, maybe he was a tad overprotective, keeping her by his side at every moment.

Even up until the time they arrived at a small airport, paying for a commute to Texas.

"I feel so special," Nina teased as Rick held her hand tight while they boarded.

He loaded their backpacks—all they had after their far too close brush with death—and looked down at her. She was sunburned, weary and bruised, and she'd never looked more beautiful. His heart squeezed. "I love you, Nina."

Her smile faded, and her eyes lit with a love that stole his breath. "I know. We are going to make it, Rick. We are." She buckled herself in, closed her eyes as they took off.

Still holding her hand, Rick craned his neck and watched the Amazon disappear.

"Is it gone yet?"

"Just about." He brought her palm to his lips.

Opening her eyes, she gave him a look that told him he was her entire world. Him. Rick Singleton. Amazing, and yet again his heart squeezed. "You will marry me, Nina, won't you?"

Her eyes widened. "Are you…asking?"

"God, yes."

Her smile was slow and sweet and full of promise. "Then I will marry you. I want nothing more. Unless of course, you happen to have chocolate on you."

"Funny." Though he'd pay a hundred bucks for a hamburger himself, fully loaded. "Let's do it now. Today."

"What, find food?"

"Get married. Make you Mrs. Nina Singleton."

"Can we land first?" Her eyes shone brilliantly. "I want to marry you in your home country. I want to raise our son in your home country. I want him to be American, like you. Strong of will and with a passionate spirit."

"As long as *she*—" He grinned and kissed her hard when she laughed. "As long as she has your heart of gold."

A couple of hours later, the pilot announced they were coming up on the American border.

Together Rick and Nina looked out the window, catching their first view of the States, their future home. As they flew into Texas, they kissed.

Sealing the deal. Forever.

HARLEQUIN
Temptation

**Wrong Bed is one of Harlequin Temptation's
sexiest miniseries. Don't miss this opportunity
to read one of these spicy books!**

**ARE YOU LONESOME TONIGHT?
by Wendy Etherington**
On sale January 2004
BACK IN THE BEDROOM by Jill Shalvis
On sale February 2004
STRANGERS IN THE NIGHT by Kristen Gabriel
On sale March 2004

Save $1.00
off any Harlequin Temptation title
belonging to the Wrong Bed miniseries

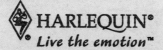

HARLEQUIN®
Live the emotion™

Visit us at www.eHarlequin.com

HARLEQUIN®
Temptation

Wrong Bed is one of Harlequin Temptation's sexiest miniseries. Don't miss this opportunity to read one of these spicy books!

ARE YOU LONESOME TONIGHT?
by Wendy Etherington
On sale January 2004
BACK IN THE BEDROOM by Jill Shalvis
On sale February 2004
STRANGERS IN THE NIGHT by Kristen Gabriel
On sale March 2004

Save $1.00

off any Harlequin Temptation title
belonging to the Wrong Bed miniseries

RETAILER: Harlequin Enterprises Ltd. will pay the face value of this coupon plus 8¢ if submitted by customer for this product only. Any other use constitutes fraud. Coupon is nonassignable. Void if taxed, prohibited or restricted by law. Void if copied. Consumer must pay any government taxes. For reimbursement submit coupons and proof of sales to: Harlequin Enterprises Ltd., P.O. Box 880478, El Paso, TX 88588-0478, U.S.A. Cash value 1/100 ¢. Valid in the U.S. only.

Coupon expires April 30, 2004. Valid at retail outlets in the U.S. only. Limit one coupon per purchase.

11119

5 65373 00076 2   (8100) 0 11119

© 2003 Harlequin Enterprises Limited
™ and ® are trademarks of Harlequin Enterprises Limited

HTCOUPHHUS

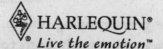

HARLEQUIN®
Live the emotion™

Visit us at www.eHarlequin.com

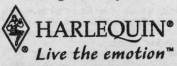

Forrester Square

LEGACIES . LIES . LOVE .

**This brand-new *Forrester Square* story
promises passion, glamour
and riveting secrets!**

Coming in January...

WORD OF HONOR

by
bestselling Harlequin Intrigue® author

DANI SINCLAIR

Hannah Richards is shocked to discover that
the son she gave up at birth is now living with
his natural father, Jack McKay. Ten years ago
Jack had not exactly been father material—
now he was raising their son.
Was a family reunion in their future?

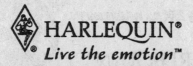

HARLEQUIN®
Live the emotion™